TAMING HER BEARS

JADE ALTERS

LEE

The whipping helicopter blades overrode the sound of the wind lashing the ocean into a fury as it circled around so close to the chopping water, it splattered up over the landing skids.

"Time to get your feet wet, seaman," yelled Darkhorse in my ear.

I crossed my arms over the inflatable life-saver, squatted at the door, and turned a somersault into the ocean below. Even through my insulated suit, I could feel the water's chill. I gasped as I came up for air, my nose red and cold. The released tube inflated automatically.

The fisherman had been treading water but was starting to panic. He'd been too long in the ocean, had swallowed too much of the salty surf that washed up over him. He saw the life-saving tube and began waving his arms up and down, drowning himself. I caught him in a half-nelson, from behind, hauling him toward the tube. Within seconds, the helicopter was hovering directly overhead, dangling a harness and ropes.

The fisherman clung to the tube, his mouth wide open

and gasping for breath, water streaming from between his lips. I wrapped the harness around him, buckled him in, and gave a thumbs up to Darkhorse before I started looking around for other survivors. Roy was harnessing in a fisherman who was barely conscious. Blood gathered around an abrasion on his head. I saw one other survivor clinging to a plank and swam over to him, shouting over the roar of the storm and the helicopter's blades, "How many were in your boat?"

I had to repeat myself before he caught it. "Four," he shouted back.

Four. Shit. I scanned the wreckage area, trying to locate another body. Nothing. They weren't more than a half-mile from shore, though. If the fourth man was a good swimmer, it was possible he had reached land. However, the weather wasn't going to make it easy to find him. Rain was pelting furiously on the ocean and steaming up a fog on the mainland. I signaled for the harness and hitched up our third fisherman.

It was a story heard often in the dark, treacherous waters where the Pacific meets the Arctic. The fishermen had been several miles from shore when the storm began moving in. They had tried to reach safety, but their skiff was buffeted with the first winds, driving it toward a treacherous underwater rock cropping. The boat ground along the edge of a sharp rock, splitting the bottom through the middle. In the storm, they hadn't been able to tell how far out to sea they were, or if there was any possibility of rescue.

"You were lucky the harbor master saw you out on the water," said Captain Josh from the pilot's seat. "He called you in."

"I hope you find Harry," said one of them miserably from under his wool blanket. "It won't be the same without him."

I put another blanket over him and handed him a cup of coffee. "You were close to shore. He could be there."

"We were wearing vests, but they got shredded up on the rocks and weren't much good anymore. Maybe Harry's came out better."

"Maybe it did. Your vests still saved you from the rocks."

You don't tell people to give up hope—not out here. Hope is the only thing that keeps everyone going. We hope for a better summer. We hope for a good hunt. We hope to survive the winter.

"I radioed for another chopper," shouted Josh toward the back. "We're taking the three of you to Valdez hospital. You need treatment for hypothermia."

They weren't well-positioned to protest. Two of them were under breathing masks. The third gentleman—the stalwart one who had clung to a piece of board and was now telling us their tragic tale—was shivering so hard, the floorboards clattered.

We had barely settled on the landing pad and delivered our fishermen to the waiting arms of the medics, and were thinking about steaks and show girls, when Captain Josh ordered us back into our seats. "Look lively, girls. They haven't found the fourth fisherman yet. We're doing a sweep of the coast."

I stifled a groan. The fickle autumn weather had left us to deal with a flurry of incidents over the past few weeks—an oil barge that had been marooned off-course, a fishing vessel that had grounded, a plane that went down near the Aleutians. The winds had a will of their own, turning and twisting and snatching things right up out of the sky. We were out on assignment more often than we were on dry shore.

"Don't worry," said Darkhorse, slapping my knee. "Cindy Moore will be there when we get back. She dances all night."

I shrugged. "She's been talking a lot of weird shit lately. She says she can't trust anyone because of Denisovich."

"Who the hell is Denisovich?"

I spread my hands, palms out. "How the fuck should I know? She can't trust me because she can't trust anyone, so she can't talk about him."

"Does she know you're Coast Guard?"

"That's just it. She doesn't trust anyone who makes a living piloting the ocean. That's just how she said it, piloting the ocean."

Darkhorse leaned back and folded his arms over his chest. "That's stark raving cuckoo."

The storm had let up enough along the coastline that the clouds were peeling back, revealing a solid wall of conifers marching up to a narrow, sandy beach. We fell quiet as we scanned the ground litter intensely, looking for a sign of the missing fisherman. We were about fifteen minutes into the sweep when Josh received a message over his headphones.

"They found him. About five miles north of here. He washed up on a shoal, unconscious but alive."

He started to turn the chopper around, but then did a wide swing. "Is that smoke?"

He was pointing at one of the nearby islands that hung like jewels in the Valdez bay. Darkhorse grabbed a pair of field binoculars and leaned out the open helicopter door, only his hand gripping the metal rail to keep him from falling. "Affirmative. That looks like smoke. We should probably get the fuck outta the way."

The captain was already starting the swing, his brow pressing into a tight furrow. "The rain would have put out the fire by now, but I want to know what caused it. That's a lot of smoke."

Captain Josh is a lunatic. The more adverse the weather, the better he likes it. We're the first responders' first respondents to the worst crises on the ocean. He swung about so sharply, Darkhorse had to pull himself in with a "whoop!" to keep from flying out the door.

"Damn, Josh," he chided. "Don't be so eager for my baptism."

The captain answered back, "Quit riding the skids like a horse."

"Can't help myself."

It was probably the truth. Darkhorse was the same way on the cutter. He would lean over the bow as far as his balance would allow and grin right into the face of old man wind. He rode the boats the way a cowboy rides his horse.

The island was primarily one dense growth of trees, with two or three seasonal shacks built close to the shore on the east side and a boat harbor to the south. The smoke was coming from the far western end. Josh eased the chopper until it was breezing just over the trees, with a clear view of the landscape below the cloud cover. There it was—a fried-out patch sitting next to a stream about a half-mile inland.

Darkhorse scanned it quickly with his binoculars. "Looks like someone's lodge burned down. Just an all-around bad luck day."

"We'll call it in," said Josh, picking up altitude and heading toward the main shore.

What happened next seemed to occur in slow motion, but felt lightning fast when thinking back to it afterward. We all heard a loud "ping" coming from the tail. Darkhorse half-stood and shouted, "What the fuck? Did we get shot at?" At the same time, Josh was fighting for control over the craft which began lurching and circling, nose to tail.

The copter tipped dangerously to its side and the ocean reared up, spinning drunkenly. We were about to do a nose-dive. "Jump!" commanded Captain Josh. "Everybody, jump."

I didn't need any more persuasion. I jumped.

$\mathcal{I}$ told Rhoda not to trust the bikers. They weren't the kind that usually hung around—road warriors on the weekends, working a nine-to-six job during the week, just using the wilderness as a playground for their bikes. There was something harder, more intense about these guys when they showed up at Pioneer Pete's, the lodge all the locals went to on the weekends to let their hair down and try again at relationships that didn't work the first time around.

Rhoda couldn't resist. The dudes had money. They had good drugs. They had kick-ass bikes that could follow a mountain goat's trail. Rhoda had short-circuit attractions when it came to men. She liked men that drove big cars and big bikes. She liked men with money. The more they flashed, the better she liked them. When the bikers asked if we wanted to take a spin, I went along, hoping to keep her out of trouble.

I cursed under my breath. I was a state trooper; I should have at least been carrying a gun. I didn't think about it at the time. I was off-duty, ready to hook up with a good-looking hunk of muscle and bone. They had all kinds in Valdez—the brawling fishermen that couldn't wait to spend their money after three months at sea; the pipeline workers with arms of steel; construction workers; fish and game. Valdez wasn't really on my beat, just a nice place to drop in on when traveling from Haines to the South Central.

What really pissed me off was that I hadn't seen this coming. I was prepared for trouble along the trail. The dudes weren't really that bad looking, they just had a way of looking narrowly at each other. They were speaking with their eyes, and it made me uneasy. My trusty Buck knife was tucked inside my boot, where it always was, and there were only two of them. I could take them both on. My dad didn't raise a wimp—he raised a ball-busting officer of the law.

But our chaperones didn't stop along the trail. They arrived at what looked like an ordinary biker's club. Several other bikes were parked in the yard, and live music was jamming inside. I thought I knew our bikers well, but apparently, they still had a few surprises for us. This spot was popular. The club was rocking like I hadn't seen since the last time I went to a Talkeetna festival.

I didn't recognize anybody there, although the girls all seemed to be from the villages. They all had that village-girl look to them: wide-eyed, overly excited, their complexions too healthy to be biker whores. That should have tipped me off, right there. The bikers always had a handful of worn-out, drug-addicted fans lurking around their clubs, willing to do anything they were asked. These girls were just innocents taking a ride in the fast lane.

I let my guard down. I mingled. I downed a couple of beers. I was beginning to enjoy myself. As a group, I've seen worse, like the fat, balding types that don't realize they no longer look twenty and the ones that forgot their toothbrushes. These guys were a little seedy, a little too cold around the edges, but the big guns were in all the right places. I started getting into the scene.

The last thing I remember was leaning against a wooden supporting beam, talking with one who seemed mildly better-looking than the others. His eyes seemed kinder, his smile more sincere. Then, I was out. Just like that.

I cursed again, struggling with the ropes. They had slipped something into my drink, just like I was a rookie. Pathetic. "We've got a lively one!" announced someone. I tried to peek through the blindfold. I knew I was on a boat. I could feel the ocean waves under me, hear the whine of the engine.

A voice answered back in Russian, then said in heavily accented English, "Take the blindfolds off. We're almost there."

Daylight streamed into my eyes and I squinted them shut. When I opened them again, I saw that we were in a large speedboat, zipping between a cluster of islands. I wasn't very familiar with the island chains. They followed the entire mainland, from the Panhandle to the Aleutians. I could be anywhere. I was sitting in the bottom of the boat, bound and gagged, with Rhoda and two other women.

"Take the rag out of their mouths, too," instructed the Russian pilot. "They can scream now. Scream all they want. Nobody will hear."

I squirmed backward as far as I could when the crewman bent over to release the gag. If only I could reach my boot, but my arms and wrists were bound too tightly. "Scream now," sneered the crewman, untying the gag. I cursed and spat in his face. He backhanded me hard enough to crack my forehead against the side of the boat.

"Not too much!" ordered the pilot. He was steering the boat toward shore, shouting over his shoulder. I saw a hand-hewn wooden pier bobbing in the water and a small fisherman's cabin. He slowed down until the engine was only a quiet mutter. In a more controlled voice, he added firmly, "No damage. We want no damage. We want perfect."

One of the girls was screaming. Rhoda and the other one were both crying in deep, despairing sobs. I blinked back tears of my own. I wasn't giving these slimeballs the satisfaction. "She thinks she's a tough girl, a real bad ass," the crewman remarked with a grin. "She'll break. They all break."

"But not for you." The pilot pulled up alongside the pier. Two men dressed much like the bikers, in leather jackets and jeans fitted tightly around the butt, came out of the cabin and rushed down to the pier to help with the tie-off. With the boat secure, the pilot picked me up and threw me over his shoulder like a sack of potatoes. "Tough girl, eh?" He made a signal with his free hand. "Let's bring them in."

There were three other girls already in the cabin, all from the party. They were also bound, hand and feet, and left discarded on the floor. The four men apparently intended to burrow in for a couple of days. A stack of firewood was piled near the door, and the pot-bellied stove in the middle of the room was crackling and pouring out heat. On top of it was a tea kettle and a pot of beans. A table in one corner was littered with junk food wrappers, fast food leftovers, and paper plates. The men wandered in and out, taking turns guarding us and eating whenever they pleased.

The pilot murmured something to the crewman, who opened a water bottle. "Anyone thirsty?"

We all were. Still hungover from the party and the effects of the drugs, we opened our mouths as obediently as baby birds. I hesitated, but the cap had been sealed. The water was clean. I let him pour it into my mouth, and it dribbled down my chin. My throat felt hot and dry. The water was soothing.

"I have to go to the bathroom," said one of the girls.

The pilot scowled but indicated with a lax hand that

someone should untie her feet and take her outside. Her guard left the door open in front of him. I scooted around to see where he was taking her. Their john was a collapsible frame and canvas porta-potty. Her guard stood in front of it until she came out, then hauled her by her elbow back to the cabin and pushed her inside. She stumbled and rolled across the floor, her feet kicking out. The guard laughed and grabbed her ankles while she squirmed helplessly.

"Oh, I'd do ya, hon. I'd do ya, but the boss says no damage." He drew her knees together and ran his hand up the soft inner thigh. "Sorry I've gotta do this. I'd rather see your legs spread wide, but this is how it goes. You're merchandise, hon. You're going to fetch a pretty penny."

He re-wrapped her ankles quickly, tightly enough for her to cry out, then chuckled and slapped her on the bottom. "It's not that bad. You might as well get used to how things are gonna be."

I glanced at the pilot who, so far, had intervened with rough play. But he only watched in amusement, clearly not at all concerned with psychological damage. We were cargo. "Anyone else like use the potty?" he asked. Despite our discomfort, we declined for as long as possible, not relishing the manhandling we would undoubtedly receive in return.

It was late in the evening when we heard the mutter of diesel engines chewing up the coastal waters, growing louder as the boat came closer. The men grew excited. They blew out the kerosene lamps and stood at the door, weapons ready. When the pilot gave the signal, they all filed out.

In the dark, I saw my chance. I rolled close to Rhoda and nuzzled at her hands. "In my boot, I have a knife. Pull it out. We'll fight our way out of here."

"I can't, Natalia." She was sobbing. "I'm afraid they'll kill us."

"Do you want to be a slave?"

"I want to live!"

I heard a series of gun shots. The girls in the room all screamed. I think I did, too. But I felt more rational as soon as I did and began listening closely. Only one volley of shots. Either someone had been taken by surprise or it had been a signal. If I was going to do something, I needed to do it now.

I couldn't get Rhoda to help, so I tried loosening the ropes on my own. I hadn't gotten very far when the men came back in. They were all stamping their feet and patting each other on the back. The pilot relit the lamps and beamed. "Your lucky day. Your ride is here."

They weren't in a hurry. They packed up gear and equipment and went over the details of their big heist, partly in English, partly in Russian. "Hey!" I shouted out. "I have to go to the bathroom."

The crewman looked at me, annoyed. "Can't it wait? There's a bathroom onboard the boat."

"No. I have to go now."

Disgusted, he threw down the pile of blankets he was holding and untied my feet. "Just hurry up, do you hear? We've got to get ahead of a gale."

He turned me around and searched my hands, then searched my boobs. I held back a grimace of disgust as his hands circled around the nipples, pinching the tips. "Go on then," he relented, pushing me forward. I went inside the canvas outhouse and pulled the curtain shut.

Squatting on the floor next to the toilet, I pulled out my knife, palming it open. I slid it under my wrists and cut through the ropes. At the back of the toilet, I sliced an L-shaped flap and peeked out. There was nobody in the woods behind the cabin. They were all at the pier, getting ready to move out. I made a long slice, sucked in my breath, and slipped out. I heard a shout and I dropped to the ground, but it wasn't about me. The captain on deck, or whoever he was, stood at the bow, ordering the men to move more quickly and get the damned girls on board. I slid backwards into the woods, eyes on the camp.

As soon as I was under cover of the trees, I began to run. I didn't have an escape plan in mind. This was an island and the only way off was by boat, but I felt if I stayed hidden long enough, they would leave, and I could somehow find a way to survive until help came. I found a tall, rugged spruce tree with lower limbs as big around as my leg. I climbed up into the branches, going as close to the top as the tree would bear without bending.

It wasn't long before I heard them pass by. Only three were searching the brush. The rest were probably guarding the girls. They passed directly under the tree. "We might as well go back. The storm is kicking up. Denisovich wants to get ahead of it."

"One more pass. If we don't find her, they'll take it out of my paycheck."

"It won't be that bad. You've got, what… six others in the bag? That's a lot of juicy fruit, my king."

"One more pass." They spread out, looped around, and met back under the tree.

They heard the long boat's whistle. "We'd better go, dude."

"And the girl?"

"She can't go anywhere. We'll burn the place down. Nobody will notice in the rain. We'll send out a skiff to pick her up when the storm is over. She'll either be dead by then, or she'll be dead when we're through with her."

DARKHORSE

I'd barely rolled my wetsuit around a change of clothing when the bones began cracking and bending along my back and thick folds of muscle and gristle rolled down my frame. A thick, shaggy coat, more insulated than any wetsuit could be, shook itself free as the waves splashed up over me. I began swimming, one powerful paw in front of the other.

I wasn't sure where the others had touched down. The waves were too high, the sky was too gray. I saw bits of useless life-preservers, far too puny for our bear-shifting forms, and the sinking helicopter, but that was all. They were bears. They would be instinctively swimming for the nearest shore. In fact, it sounded to me like a very good idea.

I could trace the island by the acrid scent of recent smoke and turned in its direction. The storm had eased, but the water was still choppy. I paddled with my head up, my eyes half-closed, my feet following my nose.

I heaved myself up on a driftwood-studded beach, its cliffs carved away by the force of the north winds. I must be getting old. That tailspin had done a number on my equilibrium. I crouched on the beach for a few seconds, waiting for the world to stabilize, then shifted back into a human. I bent over my wetsuit to pull out my clothes when I was whacked from behind. Somebody smacked me on the head with what felt like a hundred pounds of solid steel. I fell forward, vertigo completely overtaking me.

Shaking the stars out of my eyes, I looked up at a long, stout pole held in young, feminine hands. I grabbed my aching noggin, completely forgetting to cover my iniquities. "Fuck! That hurts! What the hell did you do that for?"

A stern female voice answered back, "Who are you?"

I hadn't looked up, and wasn't sure I dared. Those feminine hands looked fine and well-shaped, but they also looked like they meant business. "Lieutenant Moses Darkhorse, U.S. Coast Guard," I said, automatically reaching for my badge before remembering I was wearing no clothes.

The pole raised more threateningly, and I winced. "Please don't hit me again. I've got a splitting headache. You could have knocked me out with that thing."

"That was the idea."

I sat down and groaned. "It's a good thing I've got a thick head." The throbbing pain slowly eased and mixed in a cocktail of unnerving sensations generally associated with being shook, spun, tumbled into freezing water, and shifting into a bear. "Can I put some clothes on?"

"I guess you can." Her voice was hesitant. "Just don't try anything stupid."

I stood up slowly and shook out my wetsuit. She watched, unwavering, never once turning her head or lowering her staff. I was carrying a pair of denims and a naval-issue sweatshirt. "My badge is here," I said carefully. "In my pants."

"Pull it out and toss it over to me."

I brought out my wallet, opened it and tossed it at her

feet. She looked down for a split second. "What brought you here?"

I was busy climbing into my pants, so I gave the short version. "Smoke. We saw smoke. We were looking for a ship-wrecked fisherman and we saw smoke, so we came over here to check it out."

"In that helicopter?" She pointed to the wreckage sinking in the distance.

"In that helicopter," I confirmed sadly.

Her hearing caught a sound just seconds after mine did, which was remarkable for a human. "How many of you are there?" She raised the staff over my head again.

I cringed. "Four. All officers with the Coast Guard, Special Division Ursa." The sound in the brush was coming closer and the pole wavered intimidatingly. "Whoever is in the brush, please come out," I called loudly. "I do not want to get whacked on the head again."

Lee came forward, looking a little sheepish. "I wasn't sure how to respond, sir. If you needed assistance or if, well, you know…" He waved his finger around in the air as though it meant something.

"Petty Officer Lee Brightwater, I want you to meet…" I looked in her face for the first time, and nearly dropped over again. She had one of those Russian faces, wide across the cheeks, with blonde, waving hair that blended in with the mountainous, coastal landscape. She had acquired the deep blues and greens of the ocean in her eyes, and the blush of wild berries on her lips. I stood at my full height and puffed out my chest, trying to appear more impressive. I've never had women complain about my physique before, but when one is beating you to death while you're naked, it does make you wonder. "I don't know your name."

She held the pole in front of her and poked it at my chest. "If you're Coast Guard, why did you let the whole damned thing get out of hand? Why did you leave it all in the hands of the state troopers and the police who can't even go beyond their city limits?"

"I don't know what you're talking about."

"You don't?" She started to whack me again, then threw aside her pole. "Fuck it. You weren't even told. Did you get a message out before you went down?"

I shook my head. "Maybe we could retrieve the two-way radio. There was one on board for emergencies."

She scoffed. "How will you do that?"

The helicopter was listing, around three hundred yards out, with the tail tilted toward the water. It was only half-submerged.

"It looks like the skids grounded on some rocks or a sand bar. I could recover it."

She gave a short chuckle. "I know you guys are Coast Guard and all, but that would be pretty amazing. You can't even pilot a boat in this storm."

Now that she realized we weren't the enemy, that we were as stranded on the island as she was, she was turning soft, wistful. I smelled the changes like tracking honey to its hive. I wanted just then to crush her hair against my face and breathe her in, but instead growled, "We need to find the other two. Lee, did you see any sign of them?"

He was hovering close by, shuffling his feet and sniffing the air. "No," he said absently, then came to attention. "I believe I saw them coming in to shore due west of here. I turned this way because I heard voices."

Due west was over some rocky terrain. Over centuries, the northwestern end had been beaten and slammed by furious Arctic winds and pelting rains. The green brace of forests was claiming it with a struggle. We began picking our way through, and I had to admire the way those nicely shaped hips and that pleasantly round butt slid her weight from one side to another as she climbed up over the rocks. I still didn't know her name.

We found Roy on a bluff about five hundred yards off some mud flats. He was only half-dressed and appeared disoriented. His head cleared, though, as soon as I called his name. "Ensign Roy Stevenson. At attention."

He stood up and saluted, his pants sliding below his hips. He pulled them up on one end and continued saluting.

I waved him down. "At ease, ensign. Put your clothes on."

"Yes, sir," he said hastily. "Permission to speak freely."

"Speak away."

He fumbled with his shirt, twisting it as he slid it halfway into his pants, then pulling it out again to straighten it. "You have a girl with you."

I grunted. "I'm glad you confirmed what I thought might be a hallucination."

He looked at me from under a crop of curly, rust-colored hair. "Did she shoot down the chopper?"

"What? No! Of course, she didn't." I looked at the girl uncertainly. "You didn't, did you?"

She rolled her eyes and scoffed. "If I had a high-powered rifle, would I be hitting you with a stick?"

I decided if she could be suspicious of me, I could be suspicious of her. "How did you end up here?" I asked. "Did you burn down the cabin?"

She looked like she was getting ready to take another swing at me. "I didn't burn down anything. Denisovich's men did. They're the ones that shot at you."

Denisovich again! I was contemplating another question when we heard an earth-shattering roar that frightened a covey of ducks into scattering in all directions. The brush in front of us quaked and a giant bear sprang up from behind it, rearing on its hind legs, pawing at the air.

The girl screamed and threw herself into my arms. "Do something! Kill it! Didn't you bring a firearm?"

I tried to calm her down in a gentlemanly manner, but dude! All that soft, warm flesh pressed against my chest was causing the wild and wooly hairs to pop out all over. With a low rumble, I told her, "It's okay. I know that bear. He won't harm us."

"He won't harm us?" Timidly, she turned her head to peak at the bear. He had dropped on all fours, lowered his head, and was backing into the brush.

As much as I hated to do it, I broke away from her and turned her over to Roy and Lee for care and comfort. "I'm just going to talk to the bear, so he doesn't come back and scare you again," I said in what I thought was a reassuring voice.

She grabbed my shirt, trying to force me into staying. "You don't have to play the tough Coast Guard macho man with me. I get it. You can swim among icebergs and rescue baby walruses, but you can't just walk up and start talking to a wild bear. These things don't happen."

I took those sweet hands and set them aside, wanting more than anything to pretend I was just another helpless guy, truly in danger for my life, instead of just going to see the boss man. "Trust me. It will be all right."

I trusted Lee and Roy more than I did Captain Josh right now. He was pumping high octane. Nothing pissed him off more than losing a good helicopter, unless it was accidentally running into a beautiful dame while in bear form. I'll bet he'd gotten one whiff of her and went berserk.

His trail wasn't hard to find. He had lumbered his way through, snapping back every branch and pushing aside every sapling that had gotten in his way. When I found him, he was phasing into his human form. I waited for him to sit back with a sigh and open his wetsuit before confronting him. "What the fuck, Josh? What the hell were you thinking?"

He waved at me as though I was a gnat. "I wasn't. I wasn't damned thinking at all. I hadn't shifted yet and I heard you talking. And I heard the name Denisovich. Who the hell is Denisovich?"

"I don't know. That's what I've been trying to find out."

"And that girl." He slapped at his face repeatedly with his hands. "That girl did something to me. Her smell. It did something to me."

"We don't spend enough time in town where there are women."

Folding his arms over his chest, he grumbled the age-old Alaskan complaint, "There aren't enough women, even in town."

"That's because we don't spend enough time there. The good ones get taken while we're gone."

He pondered my words. "We've gotta change that when we get back to the mainland. Find a good woman we can come home to at the end of the day."

He was coming around. He buckled his belt and slid his hoodie, stamped with the Coast Guard emblem, over his head. "What have we got?"

"Not much to tell you until the girl talks. I think she was abducted."

We were returning by the same trail Josh had made in his head-long dash, chuckling at the spots where the grass fell over as he'd rolled in it and scrambled to his feet while in bear form. He stopped laughing to give me a sharp glance. "What makes you say that?"

"Rope burns around her wrists. And she was frightened. I don't think she gets frightened easily."

The group was just a few minutes away. Roy and Lee were standing at active attention while the girl vocalized her displeasure of their ignorance. She had found another stick, a gnarled piece of driftwood with a bulb at the end, and was beating it against the ground.

"And I told the police chief there was something strange going on. Girls were disappearing, but he told me—" She thumped the stick and stared at Ray as though it was his fault. "He told me they were just going to Anchorage. They always run away to Anchorage. But the girls were scared."

Roy nodded his agreement, his freckles standing out against his pale skin. "Lee told me the show girls were scared."

She wheeled and buttonholed poor Lee, who was too wet behind the ears to know what comes after prom night. "And what did you do about it?"

He hunched his lanky shoulders guiltily, his hair falling in his eyes. "I couldn't do anything. She told me she didn't trust anybody that worked on the water."

She saw me coming out of the corner of her eye and spun around. "That's it," she said, drawing me into the conversation. "That's how he works. He uses a clipper to transport his cargo. That's why the girls are afraid of the Coast Guard."

"A clipper?" Josh squeezed in between us and interrupted. "Are you sure it's a clipper?"

She gave him an irritated look. "Yes, it's a clipper. I've lived on the coast all my life. I know a clipper when I see one."

Josh brooded. "Let's have a look at the burned-out area. Maybe we can find some clues."

The girl held back. "What if the shooter is still there?"

He gave her a look she probably didn't understand—the look of a predator anticipating his prey. "Believe me," he growled at her. "We'll see him before he sees us." He jiggled his hands inside the pocket of his hoodie. "Maybe you should stay here. The rest of us will go out and survey the area."

Josh hadn't been exposed yet to her abuses. She turned on him, the bulbous end of her driftwood stick swinging dangerously close to his chest. "The hell I will! You're still a suspect in my case."

"Your case? Your case?" he asked with surprise.

I got between them before she had the chance to make Josh see a few stars and butterflies. "Captain Joshua Banks," I said, emphasizing the title, "may I present our mystery witness, uh..."

"Captain," she sniffed, as though finally receiving the recognition she deserved. "Natalia Ivanova, state trooper."

The way she said her name, the 'a's rolling together with the consonants like musical notes, caused my every nerve to become energy spikes running up and down my spine. I think I shall never hear a name quite so beautiful as Natalia Ivanova.

It took every bit of self-discipline to keep myself from drooling, with my tongue hanging out. Ensign Stevenson, I noticed, was not so successful. He wiped repeatedly at the side of his mouth.

"Insolent," whispered Lee, but he wasn't doing much better. He used the cuff of his shirt, pretending to cough into it.

After his surprise appearance, Captain Josh was working twice as hard at keeping his animal instincts at bay. He shook her hand and returned her formal salute, even though this was going a bit overboard. The state troopers were not a military unit. "You were on assignment?"

She didn't answer right away. Instead, she chose to start walking toward the burn site. Since it was nearly a mile away, we automatically fell in line beside her as the sensible thing to do. The hike seemed to put her more at ease.

"I was off-duty. The only thing I had on me was a knife in my boot. I was kidnapped, along with five other girls, maybe more. The cabin wasn't the center of operations, just a transport point. The abduction point was a fake bikers' club on Three Fords Road. There could be similar operations set up all through the woods."

"And their ship is a cutter… as in a Coast Guard cutter?"

"It looked like a Coast Guard cutter, Captain, but it was Denisovich at the helm."

"Who is Denisovich?"

"A mobster. A thug. A mean and nasty man. He made his first millions trafficking Russian girls to U.S. West Coast nightclubs and other establishments of entertainment. They were under his protection, but he basically owned them. He found them their jobs, their pimps, their documentation. In return, they gave him twenty percent of their income and did everything he asked them to do."

She halted and looked left and right, as though expecting her enemy to step out of the brush. I sniffed the air. Nothing but the woodland scents and the thin flavor of wafting smoke. We were getting closer. Satisfied we were alone, she continued. "He was busted about a dozen years back. They gave him ten years for human trafficking., but he was out in three and deported back to Russia, where he was supposed to stay. Now he's back, and his game is more ruthless. He's catering to a clientele that wants wholesome, naïve country girls. They don't have to be virgins, just healthy, pretty and innocent. They pay very high prices for first use."

It was a good thing she didn't see my response. She didn't see my eyes turning red with fury; nor did she see my lips curling back or hear the deep rumble in my throat, because Lee shouted at the same time, "The motherfucker! We don't have enough girls to go around as it is, and this son-of-a-bitch is stealing them? Roy, the Russians are stealing our girls!"

"And selling them," Roy reminded him grimly.

"Son-of-a-bitch." Lee did a little hop that was something like a jig, his hands stuck in his pockets and his hair falling into his eyes as he tried to make himself smaller in front of the lady than his six-foot-two frame would allow. "And the show girls think a Coast Guard captain is involved? With all due respect, Trooper Ivanova, but that just isn't true. Only a man with a death wish and a bone to pick with nature joins the Alaska Coast Guard. It's never about the money."

A gust of wind carried the smoke close enough for even Natalia to notice. Captain Josh bundled some dead branches together in the shape of a lean-to and squatted inside. "We're getting more rain. Roy, you and Lee finish up this shelter and wait here with Trooper Ivanova. Darkhorse and I will go down to the burn zone. Or are you still unconvinced we're on your side, Ms. Ivanova?"

She laughed a little nervously. "I think you are. Either that, or you are very good actors."

He barely waited for her answer but took off at a clip, with me right behind him. I could feel his urgency as much as I could feel my own. He wanted to shift. He wanted it with every cell in his body, but he wanted to talk strategy first. He stopped close to the edge of the burn, where scorched prairie grass mixed with curling black stalks of winter fireweed before being drowned by the rain. "You check the outside perimeter. I'll swim out to the chopper to see what we can salvage."

"Natalia thinks we should rescue the radio equipment."

He nodded. "Good idea. It won't work until it's completely dried out, and even then, with the salt…"

"We can clean it all up," I promised. "Just find that can of grease Roy uses all the time to keep those blades chopping. Oh, and if you find any energy bars… for the girl, you know. She might not approve of the way we go fishing."

"Do you think she approves of us at all?"

"Yeah." I checked the lump at the back of my hand. The swelling was going down. "She beat me with a stick. That's approval."

He chewed on a brush willow twig, thinking about this. "That's pretty hot." He took off his shirt. "Are you ready?"

I was ready. I couldn't strip off my clothes fast enough. The blood was pounding in my head, screaming for release, and my muscles swelled. I was bursting with eighteen-hundred pounds of vengeance. I wanted to destroy every slave trader on earth. I rose to my hind legs and tilted my head back, a huge rumble thumping first deep in my chest, then rising into my throat and exploding into the air.

had made one major error in judgment, and that error had landed me on this rock. I didn't want to make another, but it was very difficult not to trust this team. They were erratic. Alaskan women see all kinds, from near-sighted accountants to three-hundred-pound mountain men who hit town once a year, trashed every bar in it, and returned to the hills for another 360 days.

They all do their strutting, but this was more machismo than rodeo cowboys. They swaggered. They flexed their admittedly impressive muscles. Even Lee, who crouched and seemed so bashful when he spoke to me, reared up to his full height around the others, threw out his shoulders and puffed up his chest. It seemed like a lot, but it was all show. They were posturing. If they were mobsters, they would have taken me down in their first five minutes here.

Apart from being built like a calendar display of the hottest coast guards, they had heads as thick as poured concrete. With skulls like that, I doubted there was much room for anything more complicated in their emotional vocabulary than direct responses. I hit Darkhorse hard enough to make most men see Tweety Birds, and all he did was stumble and grab his head. And he was naked. Brown as a winter berry, two hundred pounds of muscle and sinew wrapped into one of the most gorgeous hunks of male anatomy I've ever seen. The trust issue was nearly completely blown away by the turned-on issue.

There was something submissive about their behavior, and that was a turn-on, too. It was the submissiveness of strong men who respected women, who would rather do harm to themselves rather than see any harm come to a woman. Lee was the one who'd finally persuaded me their concern was genuine. He was a little slow on the uptake, but his indignation was real once he understood Alaska's girls were being whisked away. A mobster couldn't have pulled it off. Not like that.

I think of the two youngest as "the boys." I know they are both a little older than me, but ages blur in a land where you know everybody for two hundred miles around on a first-name basis. They reminded me of college students working up the nerve to ask for that first date. Old enough to know how it should be done, young enough to have had no real-life experience. The boys were making the lean-to as comfortable as possible, weaving branches together until it made a nice, dry burrow against the trees. We sat in it and listened to the rain.

We had barely gotten comfortable, however, when a thunderous roar shattered the air, followed by another. I shrank between Lee and Roy, my blood turning to ice. "Two bears," I whispered hoarsely. "I didn't even know this island had bears."

"They swim," said Roy, then added quickly, "but don't worry. We're experts on bears. We can keep them away from you."

They were so self-assured, I had to say something. "Are you Davy Crockett now? I don't see any automatic weapons."

"We're better than Davy Crockett," Lee put in boastfully. "Davy Crockett can't do the things we can."

Roy reached behind me to cuff the chief petty officer's head. "Don't be an idiot. We're not Davy Crockett."

Lee shifted so Roy's hand couldn't reach him and repeated stubbornly, "We're *better* than Crockett. Could Davy Crockett break an oil barge loose from the ice and tow it fifty nautical miles to the nearest harbor? He couldn't. We can."

Despite trying to discover ill will, I laughed. "Towing a barge out of the ice is not the same as standing down a bear."

"That's right," he agreed. "It's harder."

As I said, they were erratic. I listened to them talking about the missions they had gone on until it became a lazy drone that blended with the rain. I had quit paying much attention. To hear Lee talk, they had personally hauled the towlines, not the boat, and had tracked enemies of the state hundreds of miles through the Arctic without so much as snow machines or communication devices. What amused me was that Roy didn't contradict him, not even when he said the team had once carried the victims of a plane crash seventy miles on their backs through a raging snowstorm. In fact, he'd beamed with pride.

They were cute, like butter and jam for your toast—you don't want just one or the other; you want them both. I was sure they were close to the same age, but other than that, they were completely different. Roy was Nordic, either Scandinavian or Swedish. His face was a bit round, his hair highlighted with copper tones, his eyes a mild, muted color. He thought carefully before he spoke, and when he did speak, he studied me as though he wasn't sure he had said the right thing.

Lee was Native. He wore his hair just a little too short to keep it all back in a ponytail, but he tried anyway, the locks in front dangling persistently near his eyes. He had no awkwardness around women. He had no awkwardness around anyone, as far as I could perceive. He assumed we all wanted and enjoyed the same things. This worked well enough for me, provided he didn't think everyone enjoyed deep sea diving into icy waters or whatever else this strange crew did in the frozen Arctic.

When Captain Josh and Darkhorse returned, they were carrying a flat metal tray by its handles. The tray had been piled high with items and covered with a tarp. In a rush of relief, I realized just how worried I had been in the back of my mind. They hadn't betrayed my trust, and they had come back safely. The odd part was, it hadn't been their trust I had worried about at all—it had been their safety.

They set the tray down as though presenting a treasure to the king. "What did you find?" I asked, eager for further proof these were indeed my benefactors.

Captain Josh pulled off the top. "The two-way radio, although it got a little wet. Roy needs to check it out before we fire it up. Waterproof matches. Two flashlights. First aid kit. Bunsen burner. All the blankets were wet, so I didn't bother with them. Oh, and energy bars. We keep a lot of different kinds."

I grabbed two of them without looking at the labels. "I'm starving. I can't believe you dived into the ocean in this weather." I saw Lee grinning from ear to ear. I bit into a fruity granola bar, savoring the sweet, nutty texture. "Yes," I agreed, turning to him, knowing what he was about to say. "That's better than Davy Crockett."

Their food stash included jerky, candy bars, crackers and squeeze cheese, as well. I hadn't had a bite since the day before and felt like I couldn't stop eating, but the men hardly ate at all. Since they were big, strapping guys who I knew for a fact hadn't had a meal since washing up out of the ocean, this seemed odd.

"Aren't you going to dig in?" I asked.

"We'll eat later," said Captain Josh. "We like to go fishing."

"I guess I shouldn't fill myself up too much, then, should I?" But I wondered how they went fishing; I didn't see any tackle.

Darkhorse added to the pile—a few pieces of cutlery, a motorcycle key, and a girl's silver bracelet. "Our evidence. The speed boats were gone. I don't think they'll be back until the weather clears, but they will be back. They'll want to clean the last of the evidence."

Captain Josh had started fooling around with the Bunsen burner. It was a little damp and reluctant to spark, but after a few sputters, a bright, cheery flame shone.

"The water's too choppy for light boats." He looked thoughtful. "We'll stay the night here, but tomorrow morning, I want to cross the island. There was a beachfront cabin about fourteen miles south of here. It's shelter. Radio reception will be better, as it faces Valdez." He studied me over the flame. "We can protect you better."

"What if Denisovich has control over the whole island?" I asked worriedly.

I don't know what made Captain Josh grin that way. It was nearly the same self-satisfied expression Lee had used, but more ferocious, embracing danger into his arms without a concern he could possibly lose. "He doesn't," he said, and because he gave a low belly laugh, the others laughed with him. I would say they were cocksure, except they swam away from a helicopter crash, in frigid water, as though they were stunt-diving off the coast of Hawaii. They were either the best survivalists I had ever seen or the biggest fools for having no real survival tools, such as knives or guns. And they stared down bears. The Inuit had a name for them, but I had never believed it.

The Bunsen burner was giving out just enough warmth to dry out the lean-to and make me feel like a human being again. Darkhorse draped the tarp over my shoulders and I warmed up even more. "You have an odd name," I told him conversationally. "Moses Darkhorse. This isn't horse country."

The flame reflected in his eyes danced. "My father was a Sioux, my mother a Jew. We came up here from the Dakotas when I was three."

"And you, Captain Josh?" The full belly, the warmth, and the dryness were making me sleepy.

"I was born in Kodiak. The ocean is in my veins."

My lids dropped heavily. I laid back, covered by the tarp, and began to drowse. I felt the men tuck in around me on both sides, protecting me with their body heat. It was enough at first, especially after the hours spent in the drizzling rain. It was nice to have an overhead shelter. It was nice to have warm, peaceful bodies sleeping next to me, but the wind changed, driving in colder temperatures.

Before turning in for the night, the captain had turned off the Bunsen burner to save on fuel. The new wind blew through the opening of the shelter, a draft stealing up from behind the box where the burner sat. The rain turned to snow and piled along the entrance. Shivering in my sleep, I dreamed I was lying on a frozen lake and couldn't get up. I put my hands between my legs, trying to keep them from freezing. In my dream, something soft and warm pulled me under the lake, where I fell into a pile of fur-covered cushions.

The furs were thick and luxurious. As I sank deeper, they piled around me, shielding me from the cold. The sensation was so strong, I slept deeply through the night. I woke only when I began to feel chilly again. Roy and Lee were sitting on either side of me, deep in some sort of discussion on whale language, and Darkhorse was at the Bunsen burner, frying fish for breakfast. "Did you spear them?" I asked, puzzled. I still hadn't seen any sign of fishing tackle.

"Yeah," he answered without looking up.

"Better than…" Lee murmured.

I turned to him. "Don't say it."

The fish had fried to a delicate brown by the time Captain Josh returned, carrying a bag made from fishing net. He looked very pleased with himself. "It never fails," he said. "Campers put things into the creek to stay cool and then forget about them." He opened the bag. Inside were close to a dozen canned sodas and juices.

"No beer?" asked Darkhorse with dismay.

Captain Josh shrugged, then opened a soda and guzzled it down. "They probably drank them all first. That's why they forgot about these." He burped and rubbed his belly. "Love that carbonated water. Anyway, that's not all!" He reached inside his hoodie pocket and carefully pulled out a tightly wrapped plastic bag. He unfolded it like unfolding the petals to a flower. "Eggs!"

The eggs were still in their carton. They had apparently been tied up in the plastic bag and secured to a branch, and a long piece of frayed string was attached to it. The string looked like it had been snapped instead of cut. More of their caveman-style performance. I was getting used to it. They may be the nitty-grittiest men I'd ever met, but man, were they magnificent.

If I was going to be on a wilderness island with winter kicking at the door, I'd rather be there with them than anyone else I knew. Who else would be able to drum up fish and eggs after wrecking their helicopter and spending the night in the snowstorm? A genie in a bottle couldn't do much better.

The juice was ice-cold. It was a wonder it hadn't frozen through. I sipped at it while I huddled closer to the Bunsen burner, waiting for the food to cook. Having Roy and Lee around was nice. They didn't have enough experience with women to be designing or cunning or glib. We women come by those traits early.

The older men get, the better they are at getting it down – at least you hope. Out-designing and out-maneuvering even the most cunning of women. Darkhorse and Captain Josh were older men, probably in their mid-thirties. They were high-ranking officers and they had been around. Not like men from the city, but men who'd had a few serious relationships. I instinctively put men like that on my watch list. They could be real date material, or they could be the kind you see only twice a year.

They were date material, both of them. With each fresh bite of fish, each drop of juice, I grew more aware of their resourcefulness and how completely at home they were in the wilderness. They were completely relaxed, despite the still-falling snow and wind chill. Darkhorse was the shortest of the four, although he was by no means short. The rest were over six feet tall; he was perhaps an inch or two under. You could see his Jewish heritage in the shape of his nose and chin, but his hair was blue-black and straight, and he had very light facial hair. It was a nice combination, made even nicer by my visual knowledge of his entire anatomy—plus, there was just something very appealing about a well-built man who won't defend himself against a berserk woman with a stick.

It took a little longer to thaw toward Captain Josh. He was an authority figure, and I didn't have a lot of patience for authority figures right now. I had been trying for months to push an investigation into the girls that were disappearing along the coast, but had been dismissed by the leading authorities every time. That the Coast Guard hadn't even been alerted only proved my point—it didn't make me any less angry. His recovery efforts, though, had been amazing. Because of him, I was in a lean-to made of branches. I had slept well. There was a Bunsen burner in front of me and warm food in my stomach.

Captain Josh gave us twenty minutes to digest the food, then said, "Break camp". We dismantled the branches and picked up the evidence of our overnight stay. It warmed up enough during the day for the snow to turn back to rain, but it was still icy cold and clung to the skin. It was difficult to walk. After several miles, I began to feel numb. I wasn't dressed for this much exposure. All I was wearing were my boots, jeans, and a light jacket over a knitted top. None of it was rain gear. I didn't even have a hat. The tarp I had used during the night was needed for sheltering the salvage from the chopper.

I trudged along, growing colder and less energized with each mile. I wanted to lie down. I wanted to curl up and sleep for just a little while. I wanted to be carried back into the dream of luxurious furs. I sank to my knees and refused to get up, no matter how much they shouted. Sleep was good. Sleep eased the pain.

I felt myself being picked up and placed on something warm. The luxurious furs. I embraced them, burying my arms deep into them. I slept on my stomach, my arms and legs wrapped around a rippling body of fur, my cheek resting against the velvety softness. When I woke, I was in a dark, dusty cabin that was just beginning to heat up from the fire in the wood burner. I was covered with a couple of well-worn army blankets, but no furs.

"You should have spoken up sooner," said Darkhorse. "You were suffering hypothermia."

I tried to orient myself and make sense of why there were only the two of us. "What's going on, Darkhorse?"

He looked at me in surprise. "Oh. Well, Roy and Lee are fishing, and Josh is chopping firewood. The owner left a nice crib, but he's been gone for a while. Several months, I would say; probably won't be back until spring. I found some dry cereal, if you want some, and popcorn. No butter, but there's salt."

"No, I don't mean that. You came here with no weapons. None. Not even a blade. Some of the branches the boys brought back for the lean-to were four inches thick. How did they snap them like that? How do you catch your fish? Why is it that every time I fall asleep, I feel like I'm being covered by a fur rug? And most curious of all, Darkhorse—why, when I first saw you, were your clothes rolled up in your wetsuit? Why weren't you wearing them under your wetsuit? You were naked!"

"Yes, I was, wasn't I? That was inconvenient."

"I apologize for hitting you."

"No, don't. You can't hurt my skull. It's too thick."

"So, what are you? A secret military experiment for a perfect soldier?"

"No experiment. I've always been this way."

"What way is that?"

He knocked some sand off the drying radio receiver and wiped at it with a cloth. "You'll have to ask Josh."

I didn't want to ask Captain Josh. I wanted my answer now, but I waited. I fumed and waited, stalking up to the window and peering out at the darkening sky and bleakly falling rain. I could have sworn that instead of two men fishing by the dock, I saw two bears. I shook my head and strained to see if I could find the captain by the wood pile. I made out a flickering shadow, which satisfied me, so I turned back to the pier. Lee and Roy were walking back to the house, a string of fish in each hand.

Suddenly, I didn't really want to know what they were.

The boys started the fish frying and boiled some rice they had found in the cupboard to go with it. Captain Josh brought in a load of firewood that would keep us warm all evening. The disturbing thoughts of what they could be gave way to the more pleasant aspects of who they were to me.

Rummaging around in the cupboards, Darkhorse had found several bottles of homemade cranberry wine—a thick, sweet alcohol that will knock the antlers off a moose. By the time we had gotten through the second bottle, we were all feeling a bit loopy. It seemed very funny to me, all of a sudden, that I was literally on a deserted island with four of the biggest heartthrobs a girl could imagine, posturing and pumping themselves up in front of me. Josh and Darkhorse were strutting around, shoulders back, heads held high, flexing their very impressive muscles. Lee kept breathing into his hands and smoothing back his hair.

I leaned against Roy, the quietest and the most markedly different of the four. Instead of strutting around the cabin, he was sitting next to me on the bed, playing around with a Japanese puzzle box. There were several lined up on a shelf, along with a few hand-whittled objects. The cabin owner clearly liked to keep his hands busy.

So did Roy. I leaned a little harder. He dropped his head to his chest and pushed at the puzzle pieces more intently. I grabbed his shirt just under the collar and breathed in his musky scent. It was sensory overload. My wine-addled brain burst with the full flavor of lust.

"What did the Viking say to the state trooper when he was being arrested?" I asked him, my voice slurring.

He shook his head. I tickled him under the chin,

breathing the words huskily. "Nothing. He was too drunk to notice." I laughed wildly as though I had made a terrific joke, and cocked one eye, trying to correct my double-vision. His expression could have been interpreted as alarm or intrigue. It made me feel wonderfully naughty, as though I was seducing a virgin.

"Now," I continued breathing in his ear. "If I had been that state trooper arresting a Viking, I would make sure he noticed." I pulled off my sweater top and gave him a big smile. "Don't you think he would notice?"

"I think he would notice," Roy mumbled. He dropped his puzzle to pull me into the contour of his arm. He began nuzzling my neck while his hand slid under my bra, his fingers finding the nerve endings of a nipple.

I sighed with pleasure and turned my head to look at Lee. "You, too, Lee. I think you're cute, too. Come over and kiss me."

He snuggled close on the other side, his hand unsnapping my bra, liberating my breasts for them all to see. Roy continued playing with them, holding one up to kiss its pulsing pink tip. I felt my breasts swelling, the nipples standing to full attention. "All of you. All of you. All my gorgeous men," I moaned.

I didn't know what had gotten into me. I wanted them all. I was hungry and couldn't be satisfied until I had touched and kissed and held each of them. It was as though I had been starved for love and now couldn't get enough of it. It didn't make sense. There was always someone available, but someone wasn't the same as getting off like a rocket launcher.

There was Josh, his short-cropped hair tending to curl slightly, the ocean weather already etching lines at the sides of his eyes. Even under our strange conditions, he commanded respect. He was a leader, yet around a woman, he had the sweetness of a St. Bernard puppy. He was sitting on the floor, leaning against the bed, his hand crawling deliciously between my legs. I sucked in my stomach and unzipped my pants. Grasping on both sides, he pulled them down, kissing each inch of newly exposed flesh until he came to the short-haired, golden triangle. Combing through it gently, he brushed the hair away from the opening and slipped his tongue inside. I tightened my hands into fists and felt him hold them down while he licked me.

Meanwhile, Darkhorse had finished pulling my pants away, leaving me completely naked. As soon as I had been completely stripped, they all stopped a moment to look. The sensation of having four men gaze at me in the middle of erotic foreplay made me hotter than a fire engine. I squirmed in protest and they went back to the serious business of kissing me on the face and neck, fondling my breasts and running their hands down the insides of my arms, my sides, and curving around to cup my buttocks. They left my legs free.

Darkhorse began kissing me at the ankles and working upwards, each kiss a lightning bolt traveling up my inner thighs to that fountain exploding with desire. He had gotten between my legs, his thumbs working ahead of him, kneading and pushing against the tender insides until my thighs opened wider, letting him in.

Sweet wine, how you speak to me! I was rolling shamelessly on waves of bliss. My hands slid over their taut, beautiful muscles. I tasted their salty flesh, felt it press urgently against me. I gathered them to me, bringing them inside me. I came, over and over, with each man, exploding in exquisite delight.

The night sped drunkenly on its way. One by one, we fell asleep from pure exhaustion, our arms wrapped tightly around each other. Once again, I dreamed I was covered with furs. They were the most luxurious furs imaginable, so plush, I sprawled on my stomach and pressed against the soft hides, savoring the plush feel against my nude body.

I woke slowly, curious that my dream had carried over into consciousness. I still felt I was enveloped in a pile of furs. I sat up and rubbed my eyes, then froze, paralyzed with fear. I was in a pile on the floor with four large, wild animals. I screamed and tried to scramble to my feet, but my legs were too wobbly. I sat in the pile and screamed some more.

The four bears woke up and looked at me sleepily. As they became fully awake, their eyes widened in absolute astonishment. They rolled away from me and sat back on their haunches. I waited for them to dash forward and eat me, every bone in my body rattling and quaking. Instead of lunging toward me, though, they crouched with their heads lowered and began quivering, as though ashamed. As they quivered, they groaned and whimpered, and suddenly started to shrink. Their hair disappeared. Where there had been four bears, there were now four naked men—the same naked men I had made love to the night before.

"I am never touching wine again," I announced firmly.

Captain Josh hastily pulled his pants on and began stoking up the fire in the stove. "I'm sorry. We should have told you before things happened."

"That you're bears?" I asked weakly.

"That we're shapeshifters."

"You shift into animals."

"Only bears."

They were clearly all very embarrassed. They put on their clothes without speaking, boiled water for coffee and cooked oatmeal with generous amounts of sugar. "We're going to have to do something for the owner to make up for all the stuff we're helping ourselves to," observed Roy.

Captain Josh scanned our meager belongings. "We'll leave

him the medical kit and the flashlights. And the Bunsen burner. We won't need them once we get off this island."

None of them made eye contact. I couldn't really be angry with them; they had been nothing except respectful and helpful. The whole naked party had been my idea, after all. I busied myself with cleaning the ransacked kitchen. "You know," I said, putting away a box of unopened corn flakes. "We need to talk about this."

Captain Josh gave up pretending he had things to do and sat down at the table. "I'm sorry. We didn't know how to tell you. Then, all this happened... if I had been in my right mind, I would have stopped it. We don't take advantage of women. That's not who we are."

"You can begin right there," I said. "Who are you, exactly? Or what are you? Are you mutants?"

"Mutants? No!" Josh looked offended. "My parents were both shape-shifters. It's passed on genetically and it's not exclusive among bears."

"Like Sasquatch and wolves?"

"Among others. We are protectors. We are members of the bear clan, and our faces have been carved into the totems. Don't you ever wonder why our military insignia is the bear and not some other animal?"

"I'm Russian; I'm a pragmatist. Russians like bears. Alaskans like bears. Canadians like maple leaves. That's the way the world turns."

"So, you like us?" asked Lee, with the eagerness of a young boy.

I looked at him with as much annoyance as I could gather for one so guileless. "You only scared the shit out of me three times. This last time, I nearly had a heart attack."

Lee shook his head mournfully. "Fermented cranberries will do it to us every time. We stop thinking. We turn into bears to stay warm. We over-sleep."

"I saw three brown bears and a white one."

"I'm a grizzly," volunteered Darkhorse, who always seemed pleased with delivering information about himself. "I'm from the Rockies, but I spent most of my growing years in Seward. The Alaskan Coast Guard broke up the Russian-Canadian-Alaskan fishing wars when I was a kid. I knew right then that these guys were bad asses, and that was where I wanted to be."

"I'm a brown bear," said Lee. "I was born and raised just outside Fairbanks. It was while I was studying at the University of Alaska that I decided I wanted to become a Coast Guard. I like ice breaking."

"I'm a Kodiak," Josh put in. "My people have always guarded the Aleutian waters. We helped make America safe during World War II. "

Roy blushed. "I'm a polar bear. My ancestors came over as prospectors two hundred years ago. They settled in Nome. I'm like you, Natalia—I'm native to Alaska, but I'm not a Native."

Josh waved his hand in a gesture of dismissal. "We can't all be perfect. How do you feel about us now—as a group, I mean? Are you going to choose one of us as a boyfriend, or do you just want to forget anything happened?"

Forget? I gave a short laugh that sounded more like a bark. It was impossible to forget the juiciest night of my life —and the most shocking morning. But choose a boyfriend? In Alaskan society, it was common for a woman to have more than one boyfriend. Single men were as plentiful as snowshoe rabbits, but single women were as difficult to find as gold nuggets. A lot of single women worked out their romances on a rotating basis. When the guy she was with fucked up, he went to the back of the line and number two became available.

I didn't have an assembly line, yet. I had friends. I'd dated casually, but had never fallen head over heels. At twenty-three years old, I wasn't in a hurry. I wasn't sure an assembly line was the answer—not at any time in my life, and certainly not with these fellas. They were matched to a T in terms of good looks, fabulous builds, and quirky behaviors, and they were bonded. Brotherhood-type bonded. You get in the middle of a brotherhood bond, and you become a wedge that drives them apart. Or, you can be the glue that keeps them together.

"No, I'm not going to forget it. I'm not going to choose, either. I don't want to play games. I like all of you equally. If you can accept that, so can I."

Lee did a little dance that nearly spun him crashing into me. "Are you going to give me a wallop the way you did Darkhorse?"

"If you deserve it."

"I'll try."

I had a long way to go in understanding bears.

I was trying to ignore what she was doing to me, but she brought it up herself. That first whiff of her, driving me insane before I had shifted into my human form. And the name "Denisovich" was so familiar. It nagged at me. I remembered hearing it years ago, but I couldn't remember why—only that the name provoked rage. I'd burst into the clearing where that poor girl was standing without a thought as to my appearance.

Why is the flesh so weak when it's surrounded by gristle and bone? Beginning with the first evening out in the open, when she slept at night, I kept careful watch and noticed when the cold crept in, turning her lips blue. I shifted, giving her a warm, furry rug to lay against. Longing for their own fur coats, the others had shifted, too, cradling her in their giant paws, keeping away the stealthy night that touches with deathly, frozen fingers. I knew there was a chance she would have a conscious memory of it, but we had shifted as much for her survival as our own.

It was a relief to see everything out in the open, like getting a rotten tooth pulled. We couldn't say how much longer we would be on the island. The radio had dried out, but there was still the matter of cleaning and checking all the parts to make sure there would be a good connection. If we fried the radio, someone would have to swim across to get help. Natalia would not be able to withstand the water, even if she rode on our backs.

After our initial awkward, embarrassing, and finally forthright meeting, we all went to work either patrolling the perimeter or helping Roy with his jumble of wires, circuit boards, or whatever else he needed for equipment. The sky had begun clearing by the time the radio crackled with its first signs of life. This was both a blessing and an additional worry. The clear weather meant if we carried the radio outside, we would get a stronger signal. It also meant the speed boats could come back. I hurried Roy along, wanting to get the message out ahead of the slave traders.

Roy didn't like to be hurried. He wasn't a communications specialist, but his hobby was radios. He loved them. He had been a short-wave operator on the North Slope before he could spell "Mississippi" correctly. He listened to the static as though it contained its own guidance system, turning dials, wriggling loose wires, until a faint voice answered his emergency signal. "Switch me to Coast Guard Cutter 739, Commander Peter Swenson."

More static and a rumbling voice that rode above the white noise. "Commander Swenson speaking."

I grabbed the mic from Roy. "Pete, this is Josh. No time to explain, but we're marooned on an island about seven miles west of where they picked up the stranded fishermen. I need you to bring the cutter." I gave the coordinates my best shot. "And Pete. Bring a skeleton crew. Only the most trustworthy. Bring no other personnel, enlisted or non-enlisted. You are operating under my direct orders."

"Yes, sir," he said. "Thirty minutes, sir. I'll be there inside thirty minutes."

I didn't doubt him. Pete wasn't a shapeshifter, but he was a member of a very select group that knew we were. His loyalty was unshakable. His crew would be discreet and would ask no questions. The radio sputtered and went out. Its battery was weak and there was nothing available for recharging it, but it had done what we needed it to do.

The entire time the rest of us hung around the radio, listening to the fading voice over the wire, Darkhorse had kept guard, moving restlessly from one end of the clearing to the other. I didn't pay much attention. Darkhorse had a radar that kept him on alert twenty-four seven. Half the time, however, it was sheer paranoia. I settled on the pier and waited for my boat.

Darkhorse joined me a few minutes later. "Do you hear something, Captain?"

I turned my head in the direction he indicated. In the far distance, I picked up the thin wail of a four-stroke engine. "The speed boats," I said in a low voice. "They're returning to the burn-out."

"They will be searching for Natalia."

I clenched my teeth so tightly together, my jaws ached. "They aren't going to make it this far. I'm going after them."

"I'm going with you," said Darkhorse.

I had already begun strolling toward the far edge of the clearing but turned to face him. "No, you're not. I need my lieutenant out there in front, in case the boat arrives before I get back. That's an order, sir."

"Then take Lee. He's chomping at the bit."

"Lee it is, but I'm not waiting up for him. Tell him to meet me at the lean-to."

I left Darkhorse to explain the slight change of plans to the others while I pounded through the forest as quickly as my legs would carry me. My body wanted to shift, desperately. I stopped with a groan and tore off my clothes, rolling them into a ball. I heard someone panting behind me and wheeled around.

"Reporting for duty, Captain Josh," announced Lee cheerfully.

I let out my breath in a whoosh. "Am I getting old? I had a five-minute start."

"Number one in special unit long-distance track. Your island is but a spot in the Denali region."

"All right." I placed my hand on his shoulder so he would pay close attention. The one thing that kept Lee from moving up the ranks as quickly as Ray was his astonishing selective hearing. "You circle around to the left of the burn site and I'll circle to the right. Stay in the woods, though. If they see a bear sniffing around in the open, they might shoot at it. I want to draw them far enough inland that they can't make it back to the boats."

"Do we kill them?"

"No, no. Not right away. We need information, first."

"But we will kill them."

"We arrest them." I couldn't hold back the change any longer. Hair began popping out of the engorged muscles, my snout grew long, my teeth sharp and jagged. I shook with the power of eighteen hundred pounds. A guttural call rose from my throat, startling the small, wild creatures. Branches crackling behind me, I galloped through the woods as fast as my back legs could kick my front legs forward, chewing up the land in front of me with four-inch, sharper than steel claws. I had to reach the burn site before the slave traders had time to examine it and see that Natalia had not been alone, and that the helicopter team had survived. I needed to be there before they went back to their boats.

A bear isn't the fastest land animal on earth, but at a good sprint, he can tear up some miles. I was starting to feel a little winded by the time I got a good whiff of the site. Bears are amblers. They can cover huge amounts of territory just roaming along, but they are seldom in a hurry. If you were pushing along a body as big as a freight engine, you wouldn't be in a hurry, either.

I couldn't see Lee on the other side, but I knew he was there. When I circled just right, I caught his scent.

I also caught another scent, and then another. Both human. I crept through the brush, my dark coat blending in with the shadows. Two men, both in dark, knit caps and leather jackets. They were carrying rifles but leaned against them casually as they examined the recent footsteps disturbing the site and wandering off into the forest. After a short argument, they turned toward the beach and pointed along the eastern shoreline.

It was now or never. I raced toward the beach ahead of them, then made a sharp U-turn, charging them directly from in front. They were too surprised to react quickly and took too long fumbling for their rifles. The instant the lead man had raised his weapon to his shoulder to take aim, he was bowled over by a giant ball of teeth, claws, and fur. His sidekick forgot he had a rifle at all. He dropped it, scrambled backward two feet, then bolted for the speedboat. I took off after him.

The bugger was fast, I have to hand him that. He had already fired up the engine and was headed out toward the bay when I caught up with him. Desperate, he grabbed a paddle and tried beating me on the head, which was pitiful. I've got the cranium of a brick wall. I roared and flipped the boat like it was a toy. He gasped and thrashed around in the icy water, panicking more with each passing second. I tried to rescue him. I grabbed at the back of his jacket with my teeth, thinking I would haul him to shore, but he tore his jacket loose and began swimming. I let him go about thirty yards, then pushed my front paw into the middle of his back. He spluttered, floundered like a fish with a hook in its mouth, then went under, face down. I could have brought him in, but I didn't. I swam back to shore, while the body floated gently and lifelessly on the water.

Lee still had the fearless leader pinned down. He was slobbering over him, nudging the petrified man with his snout and making woofing sounds. "I arrested him," he growled in bear language. It was impossible to speak human in bear form.

I roared into our victim's face just to watch his eyes bulge and his face turn white in terror, then shapeshifted into human form right in front of him. His mouth gaped and he tried to cry out, but no sound came. I squatted beside him. "Where is Denisovich?" I asked.

He wet his lips and croaked, "I don't know." Lee dropped some of his weight down on his prisoner's legs, causing him to moan. "Take the bear off me and I'll tell you."

Lee got up grudgingly, swatting at the slave trader's face and leaving two light shred marks. As soon as he was free, the trader rolled over and tried to escape. I tackled him and straddled his chest. "Where is Denisovich?"

"On his way to Seattle right now. We're recruiters. We stay on the mainland. We only came back to get rid of the girl."

"There's no 'we' anymore, just you. Where did Denisovich get the boat?"

"We bought it at a very good price."

I made a fist and slammed it into his jaw. "Where did he get the cutter?"

"Sitka. We picked it up in Sitka."

"Where is the captain?"

"He's dead."

I hit him again. "Who was the captain? Who was it?"

"Alan McCarthy. I didn't kill him. I'm a recruiter. I don't go out on the boats. It was Denisovich."

"But you were willing to kill a defenseless girl." The rage rumbled deep inside. Unable to hold back the change, I shifted back to bear form and slashed him again and again, the hot anger churning and boiling into my pads. The fury splattered in red hot blood. With his head rolled to one side, his body convulsed, then straightened.

"He's dead," growled Lee in bear language.

"Yeah." Two dead slave traders, either mauled by humans or mauled by bears. Forensics could sort it out. I'd gotten what I came for. "Let's go."

It was nice to amble back to the cabin. Lee was a good-looking kid, but in bear form, he was magnificent. He would never get as large as a Kodiak brown, but his shoulders had a powerful girth, accented by a golden-tipped fur collar. He was sleek, with the plush velvet coat of youth and a jaw that was only beginning to widen. He would top twelve feet someday.

The crew had been getting impatient for our return and let out a cheer that was half-jest, half-genuine when we walked back out into the clearing in our human form, pretending we had just gone for a stroll. Once we had been welcomed aboard, however, the atmosphere grew serious. My team, along with Natalia and Commander Swensen, met in the captain's cabin.

"Where to?" asked Pete.

I studied the navigation maps. "We drop the young lady off in Valdez, then we set a course for Sitka."

Natalia responded with all the good grace and decorum I had come to expect of her. "Oh, hell no! You are not leaving me alone in Valdez. Josh, we don't know who is on Denisovich's payroll. If you take me to Valdez, I'm dead. You know it's true."

"I'll stay with her," volunteered Lee.

The others were making similar offers. I lifted my hand. "Natalia is right. Valdez is too dangerous for her right now. Pete, who did you talk to before leaving base?"

"Only the harbor master when I clocked out."

"Good. Let's keep it that way. The fewer people who know where we're going, the better. Ladies, we have a crook to catch."

ROY

*I*t felt good to be onboard ship again, nice to be home. That was how it felt to me. I had family in Nome that I visited with every three months or so, when we weren't too busy with search and rescue operations or patrolling our borders. Border infractions had become fewer in recent years, although there had been a run of them shortly after the Soviet Union fell. The biggest problem these days was floating canneries trying to steal our fish, process them, and get out before we discovered them in our waters.

Most military and law enforcement divisions were busiest during the summer months when tourists flooded in by the thousands, but not the Coast Guard. Illegal entries and criminals were usually caught by the harbor master or by mainland law enforcement. Our biggest busts were in the cocaine trade, traveling port to port.

The seas were calm during the summer months, with only a few mild storms, giving the fishermen and the big cruise ships no grief. It was those iffy months between October and December that we were busiest. Boats—any boat—will push the limits to how long they can stay in the water, watching the clouds like the hands on a clock, but those storms can blow in with so little warning, you're an icicle before you see what's coming. That was when our services were needed the most.

We were the icebreakers, the toughest team in the fleet. We went into the wailing arctic zone where the sun remained over the horizon for only three months, and temperatures plunged forty degrees below zero overnight. We rescued barges, cruise ships, and fishing vessels imprisoned in ice. We had the highest success rate at arctic operations because... well, we're bears. We don't mind sub-zero temperatures. Also, because I was the only one in the fleet who can swim with ease between the ice floes.

Still, as much as I like being a bear, I also like being human. While we were on the island, our instinct had been to retain bear form as the most comfortable means of survival, but with a human in our care, we had to abide by protocol. The protocol was, no shapeshifting in front of faint-hearted citizens. The protocol had flown out the window, but it wasn't really our fault. I guess it wasn't anybody's fault. It was just three days and two nights of exposure to pouring down rain and northern winds, huddled together with the kind of woman you dream about—long-legged and blonde, her eyes taking in the entire wilderness as a backdrop for her milk-and-honey skin. We could keep up the human part during the day, but at night, we needed our blubber-rich, fur-covered hides; and when hunger struck, we needed the fish. I was just glad Natalia had gotten over it. I didn't want her thinking back on us as monsters.

Now that we were on boat, we could be fully human again, and I could appreciate the fine points. I had a marked preference for my own small cubicle on ship than a damp cave burrowed into a mountain. I don't talk much, but I do like socializing. I enjoy live music, beer, and dancing. I like sitting around a table for dinner and shooting bull. And I really like human girls. They are so soft, even when they are swinging around clubs.

I also like tinkering with things—radios, computers, cameras—which would be very hard to do with paws. After a shower and a hardy lunch, I retired to my cabin to continue working on a gaming computer for the idle hours we spent at sea. I found it more difficult to concentrate than usual. Natalia kept entering my thoughts. While we were waiting for our ship, I couldn't help thinking how sad it was that it would be over soon. I don't kid myself about things. No matter how passionate an affair a seaman has, there are few women who are willing to wait weeks, sometimes months, for him to come back to their arms, especially ones you've known only a few days.

I had come to terms with it. I was willing to let it rest, but Natalia opened her mouth. She had directly opposed the captain's decision to drop her off in Valdez, telling him, with as few expletives as possible for polite company, that he would be a dickhead to leave her behind. Josh doesn't mind being called a dunderhead. He doesn't mind being called a thick head, but to be called a dickhead was a very undesirable outcome, especially with the added threat that she would be dead if he left her behind. He agreed to keep her on board, and all the resolve I had gathered to wipe her from my mind crumbled around me like ashes.

From the look in Josh's eyes as he brushed past me, I suspected he had made the same failed resolution. "Women," he growled at me in frustration. "Are they just naturally right? Or are they right because they won't allow themselves to be wrong?"

My mouth flapped a few times before words would come out. "I don't know, sir. I know less about the whole species than you do."

He swept by, muttering to himself and waving around his hands, with Darkhorse right behind reassuring him it was all for the best. "She's a noncombatant," he growled.

Darkhorse did one of those little dance steps he used to keep up with the captain and maintain his attention. "She's a state trooper, sir!"

"Well, I hope she doesn't troop all over our investigation."

Those were the last words I heard from them before entering my cabin. I set the motherboard carefully into place and dropped in the screws. "She can troop all over me any day," I whispered.

As though listening, Natalia gave two knocks at the door, then barged in. "Oh! Is this your room? It's little. The one they gave me is bigger."

"I think they gave you senior officer quarters. We're working at half-crew."

She dismissed the information with a shrug. She tiptoed around, noticing my Klingon battle cruiser and scale model Mars cruiser. "I was curious about the way you live. You really are a nerd, aren't you? I looked in Lee's room first. All he has is a Playstation, some superhero comics, and a Janis Joplin poster. And he sleeps on a bunk."

She stood at my shoulder and peered at my work, making it difficult to concentrate. "He's a petty officer," I explained. "He usually has a roommate."

"He's been a bad boy, then?" she asked in a sultry voice. "He doesn't get a big room?" I didn't know if she was joking or not. I demagnetized my screwdriver for probably the fifth time, thinking oddly to myself, I couldn't seem to go beyond the simple act of touching it to the mat and applying it to the tiny, waiting screw. "It's his rank," I mumbled. "He needs an officer's rank."

Something told me she already knew, but she was flirting. She patted her wavy hair and fluffed it away from her shoulders. "I've never been in the military. The only boats I've been on have been fishing vessels. I think I like this life. Do you think I could join the Coast Guard?"

She blew into my face and it smelled enough like alcohol to give me a second-hand buzz. I laughed at her. "You've only been on board for two hours. That's not long enough to think you like it."

She leaned over my worktable, allowing me a peek inside the open collar of her blouse. "Josh says we won't reach Sitka until tomorrow. Until then, there's not much to do."

It was useless. I couldn't work on the computer tonight. I set the case over it so I could pay attention to my lovely company. "It's pretty calm sailing through here. Even the northerners are a snap."

"There's nothing except leisure time until then?" She dimpled when she smiled.

I was acquiring a few ideas. I locked my wrists at the back of her neck. "The commander has it covered."

Her eyes lit up and she bounced once on her toes. "Then Darkhorse is free, too? Let's go visit him."

Before I could gather my wits about me, she had taken me by the hand and was dragging me to the door. "Wait. Wait," I pleaded. "This is down time, unwinding time. Everyone likes to be alone for a few hours."

She continued tugging. "Not this time! This is let's-celebrate-because-we-got-off-that-damned-island time. C'mon, now. Party like a state trooper!"

It was only then that I noticed she had a bottle of champagne that she was shaking vigorously. "Open wide!" She giggled as she lifted her thumb and hit me with the spray. The door flung open. On the other side, Lee was laughing his dick off. He was similarly drenched and brandished three more unopened bottles.

I was astonished. "Where did you get those?"

Natalia gave me a big grin. "Pete gave them to me when I asked if there was any celebratory champagne for successful missions." She dropped her voice and whispered conspiratorially, "He gave me these from the captain's stash! I saw. It was from the cabinet on the pilot's deck." She giggled some more and tucked a hand through each of our willing elbows. "I believe he was hitting on me, but I told him I was taken." I beamed. That was a solid! Alaskan girls don't say that type of thing unless they're holding a full house.

Since she didn't think she could get anymore fizz out of the champagne after shaking it twice, it was only practical to finish the first bottle off before continuing to Darkhorse's cabin. The more I thought about it, the more I looked forward to a visit with Darkhorse. He was the boldest, the most reckless, and the captain's best friend. If anyone knew how to party, it was him.

We opened a new bottle, shook it, then waited outside while Natalia worked her magic. It didn't take him long to come bursting out, already in full swing. That man could drink a bottle of wine poured off the Eiffel Tower. He caught a considerably larger amount of the spray than I had managed and grabbed the bottle, guzzling it down. "We've got to save some for the captain," pleaded Natalia.

"How many bottles do you have left?" he asked.

"Two and what you have in your hands."

"Well, I've got to catch up with you guys, don't I? We'll finish off this one, let the captain catch up on the next one, and still have one to spare."

Darkhorse was our lieutenant. Who were we to question his decisions? We polished off what Darkhorse didn't drink of the second bottle, then popped open the third and handed it to Natalia. She knocked once at the captain's door and walked in. We waited, shuffling our feet and looking at each other expectantly. I felt we needed to get things moving before our buzz died off. "She must be having a hard time convincing him to go outside. You know how he can be about his private time."

"Oh, fuck that," said Darkhorse. "She's in there with him. That's not private. Let's go inside."

He kicked open the door, expecting Josh to be cantankerous about sharing good cheer among his fellow men, and ready to defend our rights to feeling jolly, but instead saw the captain and the lady in a very passionate embrace. "Well, shit," he said.

Lee also looked unhappy. "I guess this is the end of the party line."

I was slowly edging my way toward the exit, but Josh stopped me. "Oh, come on, white boy. You're part of the team. All of you. You're being ridiculous. We've already been on our first date."

He huddled us into a group hug. The champagne bubbled desperately under Natalia's thumb. Once freed, it exploded in a grand shower of release. This was how the state troopers partied—spraying more champagne on the outside than on the inside, screaming at grade D jokes, jumping up and down to erratic music that faded in and out of the radio. As Lee would say, they party better than Davy Crockett.

All our laughing, hugging, and spraying each other with champagne gave us a desire to lie down. I threw myself across the bed, mildly aware this was the captain's bed, large and comfortable, and this was his room, the most spacious on the ship. My ribs hurt the way they used to when my sister would tickle them too long. I was sweaty and sticky, although I had just had a shower, but I didn't care. I felt deliriously happy.

Our heads were all touching in a circle, but Natalia soon became the central focus. With no fresh women's clothing to give her when she arrived on board, she had been handed a standard set of seaman's clothes, with a button-up shirt and buttoned trousers. Natalia was a tall woman, around five-foot-nine, with broad shoulders supporting very perky breasts, a tapered waist, and hips just broad enough to balance out her shoulders. She placed curves and swells into that outfit we had never seen before in seaman's clothing.

I watched as Josh slowly slid toward her and began unbuttoning her shirt. I felt hazy and bubbly and could only watch as she turned her head and smiled at him. He peeled back the top to reveal she was no longer wearing a bra, but a men's ribbed tank. Her breasts pressed against the ribbing, the nipples straining the fabric. Idly, he ran his hand over the top of them, then slipped it under one thin strap, circling the breast and rolling the nipple. Her head lolled back, and she breathed deeply.

From above her, Darkhorse laid on his stomach and kissed her face. He took the tee-shirt and pulled it up over her arms, then pulled her arms across the back of his neck while he continued kissing her. Her exposed breasts spread below her raised arms, milky white with puffy, pink centers.

Still with a strange sense of lethargy, I slipped downwards until my knees were on the floor and turned so my head was facing her lap. Slowly, with fascination, I began unbuttoning her pants. Each tiny unveiling exposed a new treasure trove of remarkable, sun-ripened flesh, firm and energetic with country life, heaving with anticipation. I lifted her buttocks and sat underneath her to finish my slow unveiling, then laid back with my knees over the edge of the bed, pulling her down on top of me, my cock standing proud and tall between her legs.

Josh was going down on her. I cradled her breasts from behind, my thumbs and forefingers finding the lovely, upright nipples and rolling them while gasps of pleasure escaped from her throat and her breasts swelled larger and became a more bluish pink around the engorged tips. I felt the most astonishing sensation of the head of my cock nuzzling right up against her clit, the soft hair wrapped around it and a tongue licking and sucking at the edges. I was the first to lose my wad.

I collapsed, my enterprise drained, Natalia's wonderfully rounded ass ground in frustration against my unfulfilled promise. I held on to her tits, as firm as melons, the nipples throbbing. Josh climbed between her demanding legs, spreading them wider so that they draped over my knees. She raised her pelvis and he drove his hot, throbbing member into her. She moaned and tried to raise herself to embrace him, but I pressed her down as he pumped rhythmically. Screams of ecstasy burst from her throat, yet her hot little cunt remained dissatisfied.

She was held back from wrapping him up in one gigantic orgasm. While I embraced her from behind, my hands teasing and torturing her breasts, Lee and Roy held her with their ankles locked firmly against my calves, licking and nibbling at her inner thighs. When Josh came, she was still being held wide open, squirming and heaving, her crotch held high, begging for more.

Lee slipped a finger inside her and she sucked in her stomach, raising herself higher. He squeezed her little joy box. She wriggled. He opened the lips of her vagina and nuzzled the stiff, upright clit with his cock. She thrashed. "Motherfucker. Give it to me." He slid inside, eased halfway out, then buried his shaft again while she bumped and ground against him.

He refused to completely satisfy her as well. While he rode her, he continued to massage her clit while I kept her breasts erect and yearning. He pulled out just before he came, leaving her gasping and cursing. She was a red-hot tomato now. Every sensory gland in her body was screaming for release.

Darkhorse mounted her last. It was deliberate. We had each only taken a taste of her, so there would be enough to go around. She was so hot; her pussy was pulsing. He eased her frenzy, first taking her breasts and sucking at each tit until she sighed and cradled his head between them. He pulled her up into a sitting position and wrapped her legs around his back. As he entered her, she locked her legs tightly at the ankles, her back bowed. They were still on top of me. I felt her soft, round butt gliding back and forth along my limp member until it began to wake back up and ask for more.

We spent the entire night absorbed in pleasure. When we no longer had the energy to fuck, we simply curled around her, nuzzling her and fondling the beautiful, abundant parts of her, sniffing her wild honey hair and happy for a new clan member. Though she wasn't *really* clan. She was human, but a lot of shapeshifting bears have had human clan members and they had turned out all right.

DARKHORSE

To tell you the truth, I've always been a little anxious about proving myself. Although I was treated as an equal, there was one way I was an outsider and that way couldn't be changed. I wasn't born in Alaska. Even Roy, as white as the fresh-driven snow, could one-up me on that. There was another way that shouldn't bother me at all, but it did. The Alaskan big bears were considerably larger than Rocky Mountain Grizzlies. Lee wasn't that much bigger. It's probably why I've always felt a close rapport with him. The Denali brown bear isn't much different than a grizzly. Lee isn't extremely fond of diving into the ocean, but he loves to run, and he loves doing dangerous things. See? Not much different at all than a grizzly.

But Kodiaks and polar bears? Holy motherload! I've heard the shape-shifter circle debate sometimes over who would come up winner in a competition. Polar bears swim better, and pound for pound they are well-matched in size with the Kodiak, but for sheer ferocity, I'd say the Kodiak would come out on top.

Roy kept his calm nearly all the time. He calculated, but

his calculations were too slow. For all his firecracker temper, Josh went straight for the jugular vein—without hesitation, without thought. That may sound reckless, except Kodiaks don't have a vulnerable spot on them. Their layers of fat are so thick, it would take a hand grenade to do real damage.

Fortunately, at a young age, I began to understand respect didn't depend on size and strength as much as it did courage, perseverance, and the willingness to help others. Before I finished high school, I knew what I wanted to do and joined the Coast Guard right after spring graduation. I never regretted it. I needed something that could make use of my special abilities and the recruiter who dealt with shapeshifter placement knew just what to do.

Alan McCarthy had been my trainer. He wasn't a shapeshifter, but he had worked with them. I liked to show off around him just to see him roll his eyes and tell me someday I was going to take a nose-dive into shark-infested waters. He liked to hope for the worst, believing it would inspire me to do my best. When I heard he was dead, I wanted to shred the island to pieces. It wouldn't have done any good, but my bear instincts still rumbled to knock over some dead trees and tear up a few hills. I was glad to hear the captain had killed the two slave traders, but I still seethed with my own taste for revenge.

Natalia saved me. I was going to drink myself silly with a bottle of Jack Daniels that I kept in the closet, with no intention to sober up until we arrived at port. I was preparing myself for this long deliberation with the dark spirits when Natalia waltzed in. She was freshly showered, her hair pulled back in a loose ponytail, her eyes sparkling. She was half-drunk. Rather than climb inside a bottle and pull the gloom and doom in with me, there was a shiny and spontaneous new life right ahead.

She saved all of us. We were vibrating with anger. Even

the skeleton crew, all familiar with our shape-shifting ways, were uneasy around us. It's probably why Pete surrendered the champagne so willingly. He understood. Coast guard was family and he was angry, too, but at least he didn't have to worry about uncontrollably breaking out in fur and claws. Anything to make the shifters happy was a logical course of action.

Natalia put out the fire. The anger was still there, crackling at the backs of our minds, but our heads were cool, our bodies exhausted. Instead of fury, we slept in the sweet innocence of pleasure. You've got to love a woman like that. You've got to love the way she loves us.

If we weren't the most polite and civilized people on the planet by the next morning, at least we were loud, cheerful, and had hardy appetites. This relieved everyone in general. By noon, the tiny port town of Sitka was shining in the distance. In this part of the Panhandle, the islands are like exquisite jewels laced together for a necklace. The wildlife was so intense, it made my nostrils flare. I sneaked off the boat once just to dive with the seals. I had become so accustomed to freezing temperatures that I didn't need to shift in order to swim these warmer waters. All I needed was my wetsuit.

When I had dressed and returned to the Captain's deck, Josh was contacting the harbor master. After sending him his identity code, he asked if there had been any news concerning Captain McCarthy. The answer was given in the slack voice of someone who was enjoying the lazy winter traffic. "McCarthy? He went on vacation. I haven't seen him in about three weeks."

I stood intently beside Josh to listen. "Has his boat been out?" Josh asked.

"No, I don't think so." I could hear the squeak of a drawer opening, the sharp shuffle of papers, then a tapping sound.

The harbor master cleared his throat. "This is odd. A Lieutenant Rawlings took it out two weeks ago. No return dates. The documents are all signed and stamped. I don't know how I missed this."

Josh was clenching and unclenching his fists. I could swear the curly hairs on his chest were growing longer and thicker. I took the mic so he wouldn't sprout fangs. "Harbor master, can you tell us where McCarthy was vacationing?"

"Sure. That's a no-brainer. He has a lodge just a few miles outside Ketchikan. Real nice place. He and a few other officers were going there for rest and recreation."

I glanced at Josh. The sweat was trickling down his brow, but he had calmed down. "Harbor master, we're docking at the Coast Guard auxiliary pier. Can you meet us at fourteen hundred hours? Bring the documents with you."

The boat docked into a nearly deserted port. Everything slowed down in winter; tourism, commerce. Some locals strolled the piers and others dropped crab traps over the side, taking advantage of the peaceful slow season when the sea life crept under the docks to scavenge scraps left by the fishing boats.

We met in the ready room. The cook had been instructed to set out coffee and sandwiches as a gesture of our hospitality. That's one thing I admired about Josh. He was a hell of a diplomat. He always knew just what to say and do to keep information channels running smoothly.

The harbor master was as lean and gnarled as the old growth willow that twisted and turned in the wind. He had long, grey hair that straggled out of a ponytail, and shrewd, blue eyes. He was a seaman, through and through. Josh studied the documents in front of him, rubbing the stubbly beard he had failed to shave away that morning. I never understood why he could grow a full beard when I couldn't, as Jews were not known for their hairlessness.

Josh wasn't full Native, I knew, but I still considered it a mystery.

Josh clasped his hands together and managed to look very sad and regretful. "Harbor master, I need to fax these documents to headquarters. They could be counterfeit."

The harbor master was a smoker and wanted a cigarette badly. He tapped two fingers against the table and said, "Honestly, I don't remember how they got there. I don't remember logging out 'Christina.' The documents are all there, but I swear I didn't sign them. That looks like my signature, but it isn't."

I could feel the harbor master's discomfort so much, I felt bad. I shoved the plate of sandwiches at him and he took one, nibbling at it without interest. His eyes down, Josh muttered, "We have a hand-writing expert on board."

He turned the paperwork over to Pete to be faxed. The harbor master had torn his sandwich apart in bitter pieces but had not eaten much of it. "Go ahead and have a smoke on deck," invited Josh. "There will be a record with the admiralty if *Christina* was authorized to travel under a lieutenant commander. In the meantime, you are not to discuss this with anyone."

The harbor master nodded and went outside, lighting up with obvious relief. I followed him out, as much out of sympathy as wanting to get a measurement of his loyalty. "Do you know McCarthy well?"

He nodded, inhaling deeply and letting it out through his nose. "He likes to play cribbage. On quiet nights, he'll come over to the office and we'll play cribbage. He brought me a nice scrimshaw cribbage board one year. Still have it. I keep it on the shelf up over my desk. Beautiful board. It has caribou carved on it."

"Did he say anything about missing girls?"

"There's been some discussion. You hear it. A girl missing

here. One there. It's common talk, though, lieutenant. I don't know how much stock McCarthy put in it."

"And you?"

The harbor master put out his cigarette and threw it in the trash container. "I don't know. They run off and sometimes, they don't want to be found. But then, sometimes, they need to be found. How am I to know the difference? I'm not a detective."

When we returned to the ready room, Josh was waiting. Indicating we should sit back down, he asked, "Ensign Stevenson, what do you have?"

Roy looked up from a magnifying glass. As much as he likes to tinker with things and pays mind-numbing attention to small details, I should have known he'd be a handwriting expert. "This log-out doesn't match the other harbor master signatures. It's good, but the harbor master's lowercase letters have long, sharp points. The forger tried to make them as long, but hesitated before finishing the loop, so that it wriggles instead of one straight mark. Also, the letter "a" is slanted toward the left. The harbor master makes his a's consistently upright. It's a forgery. The forger probably broke into the office after hours."

The harbor master's face was starting to grow as grey and grim as his hair. His eyes narrowed into cold, blue slits and his lips turned under as he spoke. "Has something happened to McCarthy?"

Josh stood up impatiently and walked briskly toward the door, waiting for an answer from Pete, then wheeled back around and placed his hands flatly on the table. "We think he's dead."

The poor man had to know the words were coming, but his face still blanched. "The ornery old cuss. What did he get himself into?"

Josh continued to brace himself against the table. "I don't

think it's a matter of what he got himself into as it is what someone got him into. We have reason to believe he was murdered."

I didn't think the man's face could grow any whiter, but it did. He whispered in an awful voice, "And his mates?" He noticed us giving quick glances to each other and cleared his throat. "There were three of 'em went out to Ketchikan: the captain, his commander, and his first lieutenant. Isn't none of them been back."

Three top-ranking Coast Guard officers from the cream of the fleet. If we didn't put out the fuse quick, this could turn into an international incident. Pete's smart, hard-heeled officer shoes rang over the steel-reinforced floor. "The Coast Guard left no instructions for Lieutenant Rawlings to take out cutter #374. The boat has gone AWOL. Uh, they request that you pursue, sir."

For once, making himself useful, Lee was jumping around, refilling the coffee cups. I sipped at mine cautiously. Piping hot and bitter black, just the way I liked it. The harbor master was trying to regain his composure. He sat erect as a soldier; his hands clasped in front of him. "What can I do to help, Captain?"

Josh, however, had already wandered from the room, probably to speak to the admiral himself. I sighed and shoved a clipboard in front of him. "Start by giving us the exact coordinates to McCarthy's lodge and a detailed description of the land layout."

While he was drawing out his maps, Josh returned with two zip-lock bags and set them on the table. "We're tracking a ruthless killer who abducts village girls and sells them on the black market. This is the evidence we have on them to date. This key belongs to a member of a fake motorcycle gang who lured young women into the back woods. This silver bracelet belongs to one of the victims."

He gasped when he saw the bauble, meant for a slender, feminine wrist. Tears rolled down the harbor master's face. "I have young daughters. I'd kill the man who hurt one. I want you to get those bastards. Our babies…" His voice broke and he added savagely, "I want you to get them for McCarthy, and mostly, for those little girls. How did you find out? About McCarthy, I mean?"

I patted him on the back consolingly, giving him a grim, ironic smile. "A remarkable stroke of luck. We were on an island when we ran into two of the slave traders. They had been mauled by bears, but they made a confession before they died. Karma can be remarkable."

The harbor master grunted and wiped at his eyes. "With a little luck, they'll all get mauled by bears. Tell me who to look out for. I can put together a citizen's patrol in an instant."

"No, harbor master," said Josh gently. "This is as far as it goes. Keep your daughters close to home. Be on the lookout for strangers traveling in groups of three or four, young men with strong builds and an attitude. They've been working the mainland coast, but if they've dropped down, they might hit some of the island villages. Don't engage them, but notify the Coast Guard Admiralty. Nobody else."

"I can tell the others to be on the lookout?"

"Yes. You can let them know there are slave traders on the coast. Tell them what I told you. They might be posing as members of a motorcycle gang or as oil workers. They will probably be dressed in dark clothing."

"That would be half the fellas that come through here."

"I know. I'm sorry I can't tell you more than that."

"And about McCarthy? What do I say?"

Josh was having a hard time looking the harbor master in the eye. Protocol placed him on a suspect's list, but common sense said this man was aching for the loss of his best friend. He mumbled without looking up, "Don't say anything until it's official. If we find McCarthy, you'll be the first to know."

The harbor master fumbled with his cap, then placed it on his head, turning to the captain in a half-salute. "I'm glad he didn't have a wife. The others did. They were going to meet with them in Seattle."

"We still don't know anything yet, Harbor Master."

"Yes, sir." He stood at the exit door hesitantly. "I don't have a good feeling about this, though. A Coast Guard cutter, those don't just vanish."

"No, they don't."

After he left, I sighed and leaned back. "Can Natalia come out now? She's been hanging out in the control room, listening, the entire time."

She flounced in without anyone's permission and flung herself into a chair, pouting. "Thanks for making me a part of the discussion."

Josh groaned. "C'mere. C'mere." He made her sit on his lap a minute while he kissed her and stroked her head like he was petting a bird. "We weren't shutting you out. Darkhorse, explain it to her."

I took her hands. "You're off the mainland, now. If these island people learn the man behind the abductions is a Russian, they'll rip apart every Russian that comes into port. What do you think will happen then?"

"Bad relations on top of already bad relations?"

I sniffed. "A *lot* of bad relations. The traders will appeal to Canada for asylum. The islands line up with the Canadian border. Same thing if they get wind we've got a witness and some cutlery that just might provide some hot little finger-prints. They'll just slip into Canada. Then, what are we going to do?"

"If they do that, we'll never get Denisovich. He wasn't

with the others. He stayed on the ship, and I was never on that ship."

"There you go. The first line of defense is to prevent wars. This is a hot one in the making. We need to get to Denisovich before he can act, before he can cross over into Canada. If he senses things are going wrong, he'll disappear. We have one strong point on our side. He doesn't know what happened in Valdez. He doesn't know we have you. As long as the harbor master stays quiet, Denisovich won't know he lost two of his men."

"Meaning he will continue his plan."

"If he's in Ketchikan, he could be in Canadian waters, halfway to Russia before we catch sight of the island if he receives one whiff things went south. We have to make him believe nobody is on his tail. We've got to catch up with him while he is still in our jurisdiction."

She stood up and went to the window. The cutter was purring smoothly through the blue waters, sea otters floating along beside it on their backs, waiting for treats. I could tell she was in a turmoil. Her blue-green eyes were cloudy, and her fingers tapped continuously against her thigh. Embracing her from behind, I nuzzled her neck. No perfume was as delightful as the sweet natural scent of her freshly-washed hair and skin. I inhaled deeply. She patted my arm, as though she was the one comforting me. "It's the girls. Thinking about them in that despicable man's hands. If we put out an all-alert, we could find them quickly."

There was music floating in from someone's quarters and I swayed with it, rocking her back and forth. "Natalia, you said yourself you didn't know who could be trusted in Valdez. Who do you think can be trusted along the entire coast? There are a lot of ports that can be infiltrated. This could be a national security issue." I nuzzled more deeply against her neck. "You don't run rabidly through the streets screaming that the sky is falling unless you're holding a piece of the sky."

She giggled. "How did you do that? It's a ridiculous analogy."

"Yes, it is," I agreed, and hummed to the music.

"I hope they do all get mauled by bears," she said viciously. "I hope they get cuffed and slashed, and when the life has been mauled out of them, they get torn to shreds."

My embrace slipped down to the soft crease of her inner thighs. "Bloodthirsty little woman, aren't you? I like that."

I would have liked to have taken the exploration further, but I was interrupted by a rude voice. "You're on watch," said Josh, steering me toward the pilot's cabin. "We'll arrive at our destination in two hours. You have the helm."

I blew kisses at her. "He did that on purpose. Remember, whatever he gets, I get some, too."

She gave me a big, Hollywood-girl smile. "Even if it's a beating?"

"Especially if it's a beating."

I went up the cabin steps to relieve the commander, and Natalia followed me in. I sighed. "As much as I would like, I really can't play doctors and nurses right now. When I'm on the captain's deck, I'm serious. I have responsibilities to a crew."

She stood next to me at the wheel, with its high overhead view of the ship's passage. "I know that." She peered intently ahead, her eyes seeking a passing boat, a structure that would provide answers. "I'm really not into playing around. Not now. Not this close to our target." She laughed nervously. "I'm on pins and needles, actually."

To prove just how anxious she was, she walked rapidly

around the cabin then rushed back to my side and said in a low, urgent voice, "I need a gun."

I felt the hairs crawling up the back of my neck and took a deep breath. Just one look at her face told me what she was thinking about. "No, you don't. You're not coming on land," I said tersely.

She was going into combat mode and there wasn't so much as a harbor seal out in the water to distract her. "Yes, I am," she said, leaning so she was nearly shouting in my ear. "I know this is a military operation, but it is also a criminal investigation within the State of Alaska. I am a state trooper. I investigate criminal activity. I'm licensed to carry a gun."

"Natalia, you are our witness. It's too dangerous. You know we can't take any risks with you. That's insane."

"I am authorized by the state."

Even though we weren't close to Ketchikan, I picked up the binoculars and scrutinized the islands as we went past them. Here, they were like a jigsaw puzzle, with ribbons of water separating the pieces. "You need to take it up with Josh. He's the captain."

She threw her arms in the air and pouted. "He already said no." She waited for me to say something, maybe give a gasp of indignation, but I kept my eyes firmly on my navigational equipment.

"Fine," she snapped. "You want to play it that way? You're in violation of state law. I demand to be allowed to assist in the investigation or I will file a report that I was hindered from observing the evidence."

The backs of my wrists were beginning to feel furry and I swallowed mightily. There was only one thing I could do. I hit the com button. "Captain, you'd better come in here. We have a problem."

He was up the steps in seconds. "Did you see something?"

I pursed my lips. "No. It's Natalia. She's threatening to tell the state if we don't let her assist with the investigation."

"Just a minute," he said. There was a great deal of urgency in his eyes, and I knew exactly what that urgency meant. He began running to the lower deck, ripping off his clothes, until he reached the leeward guardrails. Completely naked, but with the hair starting to sprout from his limbs and back, he jumped over the rails.

Pete peered through the window, surprised but not shocked. "What was that all about?" he asked.

"Woman trouble," I grumbled as I shoved my way past him, tearing away my shirt and knocking off my shoes. I barely made it to the guardrails when I shifted. I leapt into the water. fully bear, terrifying the surrounding fish and marine mammals.

Although all bears can swim, only polar bears find it enjoyable. We paddled around in the water, circling the boat until our more rational sides took over. Or at least the sides that didn't explode into eighteen hundred pounds of flesh. Eighteen hundred for heavy-weight Josh. Twelve hundred for me. We shifted back to human form in the water. It was warmer than the Valdez storm, but it still felt cold to an unprotected body. We pulled ourselves up the rope ladder before we began to get stomach cramps.

Natalia was waiting for us on the main deck. "Well?" she asked, tapping her foot.

Josh stormed into the locker room and returned a few seconds later, carrying a M4 Carbine. "Can you shoot one of these?"

She nodded. "I can."

He shoved it at her. "Take it."

I whistled when she walked away. "She beat us."

He was watching her butt swaying back and forth as she

moved down the hall. "She's a mama bear. Did you see the bright spot?"

"On her stomach? How could you miss it?"

"What do you say?"

"She's a mama bear."

NATALIA

$\mathcal{I}$t was insane. I had always criticized my friends for having lineups, but this wasn't even a line. I loved these four men with every inch of my heart and couldn't really put one above the other. I think that was the way they wanted it, equally, which endeared me more deeply, but son-of-a-bitch, they kept their passions at high volume. Even during sex, they activated the nuclear settings until I exploded into surreal realms of insatiable desires and pleasures. And now, what was this? Every time we argued, they were going to turn into bears? You know, I must have been a little insane to accept this situation. There was Pete, a perfectly normal human male with a good career ahead of him, and some obvious puppy-dog beams of adoration, but no pizzazz. No high-voltage chemistry readings.

They let me have a gun. Damn, they don't give these things out to state troopers, but I didn't bother to tell them. I've handled plenty of rifles, pistols and revolvers. I could handle this, too. I suited up, feeling confident.

The landing party consisted only of four bears, two human enlisted personnel and me. They probably wouldn't have sent any humans in if I hadn't come along, but for anyone watching, it would look strange to see a single state trooper stalking the woods with a carbine, with no other company than some ambling wildlife.

The lodge was a seaman's dream come true. It was set up on a grassy knoll with a backdrop of forested hills and a deep rolling lawn splashing down the side of a slope, reaching a discreet, sandy beach. The lodge spread out with giant windows facing the sea and a tower perched over one corner.

A huge satellite dish was mounted to the top of the building. There was a boat pier, but no boat in sight. There was also a hangar for a plane, but the plane itself was resting on its skis, tied to the pier. I looked inside the cockpit. The toggle appeared to have been tampered with. It was loose, and there were scratches around the starter. Someone must have tried to start the plane without a key and didn't know about the safety switch. Cessna's can be tough that way.

I felt the hairs at the back of my neck prickle and I held my weapon higher, my eyes trying vainly to stretch outwards. That tower was a perfect observational point. If somebody was there, they must have seen us by now. But the landing was eerily quiet.

I advanced forward, the two enlisted men one step ahead of me. The bears had circled around to the back of the house. If there was someone inside, trouble should start any minute. All was quiet. I took another step, my heart hammering wildly. A whistle high above startled me and I looked up. Darkhorse was sitting in the open tower window, waving. "All's clear."

I let out my breath and looked down at my hands, which were visibly shaking. I didn't know if it was from relief or fear. I didn't want to make an emotional outburst, but when I saw my four lovers come out the door in their human form, I felt tears in my eyes and ran into their arms. "Is this befitting state trooper behavior?" asked Josh, feigning surprise.

"Oh, yes." I wiped at my cheeks.

"Well, Trooper. We still have one more job. We've got to check the hangar."

There was a sound of dread in his words that caused little alarm bells to go off in my head. "What do you think might be in the hangar?"

From the way he guided me, with Darkhorse taking my free arm, and the others flanking me on both sides, I knew the answer. "There weren't any bodies in the house," Josh said tightly. "Zilch. Nada. But there was blood. And somebody, a lot of people, had been living there until a few days ago. All the beds are unmade, trash baskets are full. There's still fresh food in the refrigerator. The house is trashed—dirty dishes, clothes and towels on the bathroom floor, cigarette butts and beer cans strewn everywhere. We'll call in a forensics team, but we still have to look in the hangar."

"They didn't worry about leaving evidence behind," I remarked.

"Because they plan to be in international waters," said Josh positively.

Before we reached the hangar doors, Lee broke away and turned his head. "I smell death."

If possible, Roy turned paler than usual. "I smell it, too."

Josh halted and looked at me sternly. "Are you sure you want to go through with this?"

I nodded. "All right," he sighed. "Lead the way, Commander."

Darkhorse opened the hangar doors. The stench rolled out, nauseating me. I gagged, water streaming from my eyes. I gagged again as I walked, blinking, into the shadowy building. Stretched out in a row on the floor were four dead men in their pajamas or underwear, their bodies arranged neat and straight, their heads turned in the same direction. Each of them had his throat slashed.

"They were murdered in their sleep," said Darkhorse bitterly. They had been murdered, drained of their blood, dragged out to the hangar, and uniformly arranged that way.

I reeled back against a wall to steady myself. I'd been on a few hard cases, but this was ice cold. This was the impassionate display of a calculating man who used any means to justify an end goal, including horror. A man who placed absolutely no value on human life.

"Denisovich is a coward," said Lee, taking my hands. "He murders people when they are defenseless."

He started to steer me away, then stopped. "Do you hear that?"

I gave him a bitter smile. "I don't think my senses are as good as yours."

"I heard something. Captain, I heard something at the back of the hangar."

Josh was still studying the four bodies and the faint blood trail that led to the door. Darkhorse was taking photos. He pointed out some footprints for Darkhorse to photograph, then turned to Lee long enough to say, "Check it out."

If Josh didn't have confidence in me, he certainly had it in his men. It seemed unfair. It wasn't my fault I couldn't morph into eighteen hundred pounds of man-eating jaws.

Lee began trotting off purposefully, so I followed. If there was a new development in this case, I wasn't going to be the last to know. It still chafed me a little that they'd withheld information to the Sitka harbor master. Maybe erring on the side of caution was the best thing to do this close to the border, but I felt if departments had been more candid with each other from the beginning, maybe things wouldn't have gotten so out of hand.

I could tell he was depending on his heightened senses to

track the sound. "Is it dangerous?" I asked, holding my carbine ready.

He sniffed the air. "No. It's young—a young girl."

The hangar was lit only by the daylight shining weakly through the doors. The far corners remained in shadow. I advanced toward the dark end, weapon to the shoulder, and just made out a dark form pressed against the wall. As I moved closer and adjusted my eyes to the lighting, it slowly acquired definition. I first made out an old army cot without a mattress flush with the corner of one wall. There was something on the bed, but the odd shape made it difficult to tell what it was. I crept over, easing my weapon down. There was no need for it. The shape was a woman lying flat on the bare springs, her hands tied to the headposts, her legs spread, her ankles lashed to the bottom posts of the cot. Other than a gag around her mouth, she was completely naked.

She was so pale and still, I thought at first she might be dead, until she whimpered and struggled weakly. Throwing all caution to the wind, I set the carbine on the floor and rushed to her side, then whipped out my knife and began cutting away the ropes. Lee hovered over me, blocking what little light reached in from the hangar doors. "Don't just stand there," I told him crossly. "Do something."

"Blankets," he said, blinking and snapping to attention. The two enlisted men had followed us a few feet behind. Throwing back his shoulders and straightening his shirt, he instructed them to run back to the house and bring clothing and covers for the victim. In the meantime, I had removed her gag, cut her wrists loose, and was slowly drawing her arms to her sides. She panted and cried hoarsely in pain as the blood rushed back into her limbs and I massaged them gently. She grabbed the front of my blouse, her teeth grinding together as noiseless sobs filled her throat. She wouldn't let go. I folded her into my arms, covering her as best I could. "Cut her ankles loose," I told Lee.

When he did, the girl—for that was what she was, not a woman—couldn't even move her legs at first. Gently, I drew her knees together. Dragging them up, she curled in my lap like a child. Lee whipped off his field jacket and spread it over her. "I gave an order," he said proudly, sitting next to me on the bed.

Over the top of the jacket, I was rubbing her back soothingly while I rocked the shivering girl back and forth. "You're supposed to give orders," I scoffed. "You're a petty officer."

He was being silly for the sake of the girl. Her mouth was red and swollen, her lips cracked from the gag and the gag itself wet with saliva. It must have been in her mouth at least twenty-four hours. Her wrists also showed the signs of long-term restraint. They were raw and badly scraped from struggling. She had squeezed her eyes shut when she'd climbed up on my lap, but she opened them to study him briefly. Something approaching a smile crossed her face.

Lee was still pleased with himself. "But I don't usually have a chance. The captain's always around."

"The captain is investigating. Let him investigate."

I unsnapped the water bottle from my waist and trickled a little liquid on her tongue. She licked at it and I gave her a few drops more. "They raped me," she forced through her lips, her body shuddering. "The eyes. The eyes watched while they raped."

Lee glanced toward the dead men. All the heads had been turned toward the back of the hangar, their blank eyes staring, mouths gaping in horror. Lee rumbled, his chest hair thickening. "Outside with it," I warned.

He decided he could control himself, especially since the enlisted men had returned with blankets. I wrapped the girl up like a baby in bunting, murmuring soothing words to her, although the real thoughts in my head would have made a sailor cringe. She couldn't have been more than seventeen. She had the high-boned, blushing cheeks of the Haida. If we'd lost her, she would have been just one more missing indigenous person. She deserved more. She deserved much more. I rocked her gently, listening to the terrible soundlessness heaving up from her chest.

I felt almost reluctant to turn her over to Lee. I understood what she had been through, and she needed reassurance. She needed someone to hold onto, and right now, she was clinging to me. With his magnificent shoulders and powerhouse arms, however, Lee was far better equipped than I was to carry her down to the dock and the waiting boat.

Josh had done all the investigating he felt needed doing, especially after learning we had just picked up another miracle witness. Denisovich was making a habit of leaving girls behind like breadcrumbs, never once imagining they would be found alive. If Captain Josh had not been on patrol the night they'd burned down the cabin, neither of us would have been found in time. He ordered the team back onboard, sent copies of the photos along with coordinates for the ship to the admiralty, and went to the ready room to brood. Roy and Darkhorse joined him but Lee remained in the first aid room with me while the on-board medic supplied fresh clothing and blankets for our young victim, and carefully cleaned some of her wounds.

The town of Ketchikan was only twenty minutes away. Pete made an emergency call to the hospital so the medics would be at the docks the minute our feet touched land. Lee and I followed and stayed in the waiting room while they examined the girl and put her on life support. The attendant who came out, several hours later, was also Haida. She was nearly as tall as I was, with gray streaks in her ponytail and a pair of glasses that didn't quite fit properly on her nose. "Are you a relative?" she asked.

"No. I…" I stammered. "I'm a friend."

She turned to Lee. "But you're family."

"We have the same totem."

She gave him a penetrating stare, then made a check on her clipboard. "That'll work." She scribbled a few notes before looking back up at us. "She's badly dehydrated. We have her on life support now simply to restore her fluids. She was kept in one position for at least forty-eight hours. She has bruises over eighty percent of her body, three broken ribs, and a dislocated jaw. One more day and she wouldn't be alive."

The horror of what that girl had endured was beginning to sink in. It felt like an overflowing septic tank, giving me the same almost insurmountable desire to retch. "Is there anything else we should know?" I asked, swallowing.

"You're not family." She turned and tapped Lee on the elbow with her clipboard. "And the Athabascan and the Haida are not the same tribe."

"I'm a state trooper," I offered.

She gave me a sardonic look. "Where's your badge?"

I was frantically rummaging through my brain for a good reason why I didn't have my badge, without spilling the whole I-was-captured-while-at-a-party bag of beans, when Captain Josh and the rest of his crew clip-stepped down the hospital aisle in full dress uniform. I had never seen the captain in anything but his sloppy clothes or his bear rug, so it just didn't occur to me how knock-down gorgeous he was when he was all cleaned up. I had to whip my tongue back to keep it from hanging outside my mouth.

His effect on the attendant was just as high voltage. She clasped her clipboard primly to her chest and pulled up her glasses, and quite spontaneously lifted a hand to loosen her hair. He stopped in front of her and gave a slight bow. "Captain Joshua Banks, Coast Guard, SRS, Special Division Ursa. The young lady was picked up on a search and rescue mission. We need access to all her medical files, and we need to question her as soon as she is able to communicate." He showed her a document. "By order of the governor."

Wild horses couldn't stop her tongue from wagging now. She tucked an arm confidentially through his and explained in a deeply troubled voice, "She was raped repeatedly. We've picked up the DNA of three different men. This is consistent with the bruising made with fists and boots—three different sizes."

He patted her hand to let her know how deeply he sympathized and how reluctant he was to keep this on a purely professional level. "We'll need the DNA samples of the perpetrators. How soon can we see her?"

The gravity in her voice caused us all to draw close. "Her body will heal. She was tortured, but the injuries were not life-threatening. But mentally… she's been severely traumatized. It may be a long time before you can make any sense out of her at all." She gave me a penetrating look, as though to see if I would object. "That's why we called the shaman."

A shaman would not have been the first person I would call for a mental health issue, but the captain appeared satisfied and I'm not one to criticize people's beliefs. How could I? I was living with four shapeshifters! In some places, I could go to the looney bin for saying that. Fortunately, not in Alaska.

The captain and the attendant were still signing forms when a small, somewhat stocky man appeared seemingly out of nowhere. He had a moon-shaped face, with an upturned mouth and giant crow's feet that crinkled away from the corners of his eyes into laugh lines. He wore a sky-blue, elaborately embroidered shirt, a large ivory necklace, a bracelet made from small jade stones and a multi-colored, hand-woven belt to hold up his jeans. His long braid reached all the way down his back and his head was covered by a bowler hat sporting a single peacock feather.

"Flashy, isn't it?" he asked when he saw me studying his hat. "I was looking at these feathers in the India store down on main street and I asked myself, why be a raven or an eagle if you can be a peacock?"

"Why a peacock?" I asked. Shaman were supposed to be wise, so I expected a profound answer.

"Why not a peacock? Are you against peacocks?"

"Of course not."

"There you go," he said, apparently completely satisfied.

His attention shifted sharply to Captain Josh, then Dark-horse, Roy, and Lee. He sniffed the air and walked around them. "Hey-ya!" he said, boxing at the air next to them. The team appeared unperturbed.

"Well, that's over with," he sighed, unfolding a woven ceremonial robe that had been sitting on a chair for I didn't know how long. I hadn't seen it appear. It was decorated in the traditional bright red and black colors of the Haida.

With the robe draped over him, he did look more like a shaman. The air became quiet, the way it does when someone lights a candle. He crossed his arms and stood in the semi-circle of the team. "Bear clan, I welcome you. Your spirits will make her stronger."

I would never again dismiss the stories and legends of the spirits that wander through the north. That night was even stranger than the first time I saw a shapeshifter—not as frightening, but stranger. The room was lit only by the heart and breathing monitors next to the bedside, and by a single candle in the window. The shaman bent his knees in a shuffling dance, holding something. I couldn't quite catch what it was, but it seemed to emit a vapor so light, it was like a fleeting spirit.

The dance continued, his robe creating an odd motion picture. He chanted. The shadows flickering over the walls looked like the flight of wild geese. There was a rush of air followed by a long faint howl of the wilderness. I heard music floating up over a murmuring ocean. I heard bird calls. A forest sprang up within the shadowy dance and four massive creatures stood erect, their ears rounded, their snouts tilted to sniff the air.

The chanting lowered and grew softer. Slowly, the images melted away. The shaman stood over the girl and whispered intently, then touched her head. "She will sleep well tonight," he said, ushering us out of the room. "She will dream she is safely in the village with her family. She will dream of the things that make her happy. Tomorrow, you can ask her your important questions."

He walked with us to the exit door and lit a cigarette. After he smoked half, he handed it to Josh. "To get rid of the bad medicine," he explained, waving the smoke around. I wrinkled my nose as it hit my nostrils. He grunted. "You, too. When we pass around the little smoke, he can't tell one of us from another. We're all the same to him then."

He watched Josh take two drags then hand the cigarette to Darkhorse. Leaning leisurely against the wall, he lit another. "You are chasing a very bad man, Captain Banks. It's not for me to say," he began, lowering his voice and drawing us closer. The smoke wasn't all tobacco; it was slightly intoxicating. In the smoke-filled circle, his voice sounded like it floated from the deep hollows. "But show him no mercy. You can't hide from me. I know what you're doing. For all of us, show him no mercy."

ormally, I don't have much trouble controlling my shapeshifting, but damn, that woman gets me hot and bothered. I see her and my temperature automatically goes up sixty degrees. There are only two solutions when I'm pumping that much adrenaline: sex or shapeshifting. I prefer the sex, but there are matters of propriety, especially concerning senior officers in the Coast Guard Services and what's acceptable to the public. What I wouldn't give for the good old days when everyone was tribal, and shapeshifters were considered a hot date. You can't win them all, but I would sure like to win one argument with Natalia.

She was right. She was always right. If she hadn't come with us, we probably would have bungled it when we found the girl, especially since Lee found her first. Lee's a good kid, but he has all the tact of a musk ox. He probably would have terrified her to death before we could get her on the boat.

I didn't like it, though. I didn't like her coming ashore land. If there had been one shooter and that shooter had come close to hitting her, I think I would have ripped the entire lodge to shreds getting at him and, consequently, destroying all our evidence.

We had a lot, enough to make our case for murder in any court. I don't think Denisovich knew we were riding so closely on his tail or he would have been more careful about cleaning up. He clearly didn't think it mattered. He thought his Valdez crew had wiped up their island headquarters. He had no way of knowing, because nobody had returned to Valdez. There had been no one to sound the alarm. And since Natalia had never showed up either, there was no reason for anyone to get suspicious. At least, not right away. And right away was all that mattered.

Only one person, besides the admiral, knew our destination, and that was the Sitka harbor master. He was trustworthy. I radioed him, confirming McCarthy's death and the deaths of his top officers. I knew it would cause a major rumble, but it wasn't something we could keep under our hats forever. People needed closure.

The next morning when we went to check on our victim, she was cranked halfway into a sitting position, awake and sipping water through a straw. She drew back when she saw me, so I stopped at the door, leaving it open to reassure her. Darkhorse and Roy remained standing behind me, and only Natalia and Lee went inside the room.

The girl was more receptive toward Natalia than she was toward Lee. She turned in her bed and reached for Natalia's hands, mouthing words that would not leave her throat. Natalia knew what to do. She pulled up a chair so that she was sitting so close, her woodsy, spruce-trees-and-wildflowers scent overrode the smell of hospital antiseptics.

"It's okay," she said kindly. "You strained your throat. The doctor said it's better if you don't try to speak right now."

The large, slightly tilted dark eyes, no longer sparkling with innocence, shifted urgently as though trying to spill her story from them and hoarse sounds once more gurgled up from her throat.

"The nurse said you have been writing down what you want to say."

The girl nodded, so Natalia handed her a pad and pencil. "I'm Natalia. This is Lee. Do you mind if he is here? He's the one who found you."

She wrote down, "Silly man."

Natalia grinned. "That's the one. The doctor tells me your name is Amy and that your parents will be here this afternoon. They matched your identity to a missing person's list. You've been missing four weeks. Where did they pick you up?"

She wrote down, "Visiting in Seward."

"Was that before or after they got the Coast Guard vessel?"

"Before," she wrote. "First, I was on a big fishing boat with two other girls. We stopped once and they picked up two others. One more stop and we all transferred to the Coast Guard boat. Then to the big house and waited."

Lee stood a respectable distance behind the chair and kept his big mitts laced in front of him. "Was anyone in the big house when you got there?"

She shook her head. He lowered his voice and asked, as gently as he could, "How many girls are there?"

She wrote painstakingly, "Twelve. There were fifteen. Two died, and now I'm gone."

Natalia was becoming emotionally involved. I stepped forward to intervene, but Natalia had already asked the question. "Who died?"

The girl shrugged. She was becoming tired and the questions were starting to invoke unpleasant memories, but Natalia pressed one more time. "Why did they leave you behind?"

She wrote, "Because I escaped."

Natalia's eyes filled with tears and the big blubber bear next to her pawed at his cheeks. She leaned over the girl, taking her hands and kissing them. Restoring some of her composure, she said hoarsely, "I escaped from the group they picked up in Valdez. They abandoned me on an island. I was there with a friend named Rhoda."

"Rhoda's alive," wrote the girl. "I heard of you. We thought you were dead."

"Well, I'm not and neither are you, so we both got lucky. I know you're tired, but if you can think of anything else to share, contact me at this address."

Natalia wrote an e-mail address on the pad and the girl folded it up carefully. "Wait!" she squealed in her damaged voice as we started to leave. "I know where they're going." The effort caused her to wheeze heavily. We waited as she sucked in extra air, then breathed out, "Vancouver."

Vancouver! He had a marine class boat that could slide through the water like a fish out to sea and that could hide anywhere among the hundreds of islands along the U.S.-Canadian coastline. He had a three-day head start on us. I called the team into the ready room for a brain-storming session. Of course, Natalia joined us. You couldn't pry her loose with a crowbar.

I spread out several large maps of the island chain and leaned over them. "What have we got? We know for a fact they hit Seward and Valdez. There was one more destination before Ketchikan."

"Juneau?" suggested Natalia.

I shook my head. "Too risky."

"Glacier Bay," said Darkhorse positively. "It's ideal. Heavily forested yet close to the Southeastern hub. No one would think twice about a Coast Guard cutter."

"We know they're well-organized," added Roy. "Everything was timed. They knew when McCarthy and his team were going on vacation and where they were going. They used a fishing vessel for the first part of the operation, then transferred to the stolen cutter in Valdez."

"They had an inside man," Lee pointed out, forever one to state the obvious. "The lieutenant."

Darkhorse leaned back, folding his arms over his chest. "They'll probably ditch the cutter before entering Canadian waters. You know how ruffled the Canadians get when they see us crossing their line."

I looked at the myriad possibilities dotting the map. "Then we need to find them before that happens. We're nearly at the end of the line."

"Maybe we're too late," suggested Lee, wincing at the disagreeable thought. "They've got a head start. They weren't in a hurry when they left, which means their transport was probably already lined up. Maybe we're at the end of the line."

I allowed my bear hairs to slither out enough to prickle against my clothes. "Not until we recover the boat. The boat is U.S. property."

It was a weak loophole, but one I knew the Canadian government would back. This wasn't about fish. It was about criminals. If necessary, we would turn to Interpol, but in matters this delicate, it was better to keep as few people involved as possible. I hoped I wouldn't have to involve anyone else at all, but I knew Canada may not be as eager for our form of justice as the harbor master and the shaman. Not that I consciously planned to maim, maul, and kill anyone, but these things happened in the course of violent confrontations.

With the clock running down, we needed to take bolder action. I sent Pete and Darkhorse up in the chopper, instructing them to stay within U.S. airspace. "But keep your eyes peeled," I warned Darkhorse, shaking his oversized binoculars. "As long as the traders remain on that boat, they are on American territory." That was my way of telling him if he saw the boat in Canadian waters, boundaries be damned —we were going after it.

Natalia stood beside me on the helicopter pad, watching the chopper clear the deck then swoop over the tangled tree line, following the Tongass. I liked the way she had done her hair—all loose, with only a part of it pulled back and curly tendrils framing her face. The ocean breeze rippled it so that strands tickled her lips. There was a dark, troubled look in her eyes. Amy had haunted her. Amy was the victim she could have been. I wrapped my arm around her waist, inhaling her milk-and-honey fragrance. "We'll find the girls," I promised. "We won't abandon them."

"And Denisovich?"

"I'll get the son-of-a-bitch!"

"Hmm, keep your hair down." She leaned against me, gazing at the thunderous old-growth trees crowding up to the shores of the island. The rain was lightly pelting. These drizzling showers were just a normal part of an islander's day and didn't bother them in any way, shape, or form. "Tell me what it's like to be a shapeshifter," she asked dreamily.

I was still distracted by her fragrance and had to return to earth to consider her question. "It hurts a bit, but in a way it feels good. It's like we are naturally huge inside and when we get excited, we just start exploding outward. Sort of like an orgasm."

She bumped against me with a laugh. "That's why you are all such teases! You like the exploding action!"

I grabbed a handful of sweet, perfect ass and nuzzled her neck at the same time. "You're a good mama bear. You can take it."

"Mama bear." She moved my hand back to her waist.

Glued to her like that, when she started walking, so did I. "I didn't mean about the change so much. Of course, it would hurt. Obviously, it would hurt, your bones are doing all kinds of weird things. But what's it like to be both bear and human? Are there other types of shapeshifters?"

"To be a bear…" I chuckled. "We all have a spirit animal, Natalia. It's just that not everyone can transfer into it. Which answers the next question. There are a lot of different animal shapeshifters. They are who they are. The caribou are shy. The wolves are family-oriented. The beavers are contractors. And us bears… we know a good mama bear."

"You think my spirit animal is a bear?"

We had reached the ready room. Lee and Roy were still poring over the maps, trying to guess Denisovich's next move. "Nah," I said, sitting down with them at the table. "Maybe a wolverine or a porcupine."

She slapped my head, which felt as glorious as a kiss.

"What did you do to deserve that?" asked Lee.

It probably wasn't a good idea to provoke another attack with serious business at hand. "Never mind. Any thoughts?"

"Yeah," he said. "How would they hold a slave auction? They couldn't just port in Vancouver and start the bidding."

"It would be exclusive," agreed Roy. "We're talking big money. I think they would stay off-shore."

"They have a yacht," said Natalia suddenly. "Big money. Exclusive entertainment. They're holding the auction on a yacht."

I hit the com button. "Second Lieutenant, tell my team to keep their eyes peeled for a yacht."

"Yes, sir," the answer automatically snapped back.

I gave Natalia a perturbed look. She was right. Every instinct I had told me she was right.

DARKHORSE

Captain Josh was a shit. I saw the way he held on to Natalia as the chopper rose into the air and the two of them shrank smaller and smaller. That was okay, though. I knew enough about that apple-pie darling by now to know that her heart was big enough for all four of us. That was important to a clan. You didn't break up a clan; you joined it.

Pete didn't understand. For a while, he'd thought she was our pass-around girl and that when we became bored with her, we'd pass her on to someone else. Maybe that worked in his circles, but not in ours. We were hers for the duration. We played by Alaskan rules.

Pete was a good guy, but he had a bit of Seattle influence. Despite being on the sea for fifteen years, there was something urban about his thinking. He hated my method of scanning from the open chopper door, a single carbineer securing me by a nylon rope to the welded frame, stretching out as far as my arm would allow me without falling out. One foot on the struts, my binoculars in one hand, I had a clear, sweeping, unobstructed view. Pete mumbled about safety regulations, but he knew Captain Josh wouldn't give a damn.

Even when you're one-hundred-eighty human pounds of brawn, you can't hold that position long. I started to go back inside when I saw something flash in one corner of the binoculars. "Commander, swing her around about twenty degrees and follow the southwest spur. I saw something."

He turned the chopper as I instructed. The rain turned sideways, splattering against my binoculars and dribbling down the lenses. I gave them a quick wipe on my jeans. I was right! The tiny speck began to glimmer and grow larger. "Keep your bearings, Commander!"

I pulled myself back in and flopped excitedly in the passenger's seat of the cockpit. I grabbed the standard field glasses and looked through the window like a regular person. "There it is. You're coming up on it, sir. The *Christina*."

It caused a lump in our throats to see her abandoned like that, huddled into a small, hidden cove, the reluctant conveyor of dishonor and treachery. A terrible splotch on the record of a vessel that had given fine and noble service. Pete switched on his mic to call it in, but he had barely more than identified himself before Josh broke through. "You found it? Pete, stay in pursuit. I want you to look for a yacht."

"Roger that." Pete gave me a sour look. "More acrobatics?"

"We're losing daylight. We need to get a sighting before we go back, or we've lost them. Acrobatics are required."

Now that we knew where they had left the boat and their new destination, it was easier to plot a course. I listened to the purposeful chop of the blades as the helicopter made a wide swing into the main channel, disturbing the whitecaps that scuttled back in confusion. I held the high-powered glasses steady in a super-human attempt to discern the difference between the bright clusters of frothing waves and white, solid matter. Pete shouted above the wind, the rain, and the clattering blades, "Darkhorse, we're at half-tank. We need to turn back."

I focused on a spot that somehow looked suspicious, that didn't belong, like a tiny white fleck on an unblemished photograph. "Five more minutes. The *Ursa* is following behind us. Just give me five more minutes."

My gut feelings were trying to claw their way outside. "Forty degrees west, he's making a wide turn. He's headed toward international waters. Foot to the pedal. I need a few more hundred feet." I scrambled inside. "Stay on your mark. I've got an idea." I pawed around inside my kit and pulled out a cannon-sized camera. I grabbed a bungee cord, wrapped it around my ankles, and clipped it to the bottom of the pilot's seat.

Pete looked down at the homemade tether, an expression between alarm and annoyance working at his jaws. "What are you doing?"

"Just make sure the fucker doesn't slip. I've got an idea." I grabbed the camera and wriggled toward the door on my stomach. Sliding halfway out, I looked through the lens, searching for that tiny white spot in the distance.

Pete bellowed toward the door. "Lieutenant! I'm flying blind. I don't see anything but the ocean."

Fixing my view determinedly, I answered back, "I do. I just need you to get a little closer. Keep your bearings. We've almost got it. Drop her down about fifty feet."

I was playing the odds. From the distance, it was impossible to tell what type of boat was floating on the water. I attached the telescoping zoom lens and zeroed in. It wasn't a fishing vessel. The tiny sliver slowly began acquiring dimensions. No high, deck-top cabin, no nets. Pete's voice had acquired a whine. "Darkhorse, we're in Canadian airspace."

"Close in just a little more, Pete. Can't you see it yet?"

He paused. "Yeah, there's something out there. I'll close

the gap a little more, then we get out of here. There's nothing we can do from up here."

He had to push it to close enough distance to take the shot. We were now juggling with three balls. We were in Canadian airspace, running low on fuel, and it was turning dark. I snapped the photos, elbowed my way back in, and sprawled on the floor of the helicopter, breathing hard. "Well, that was fun," I said finally.

Pete shook his head dolefully. "You're crazy."

"At least we weren't close enough to get shot at."

It was fully dark by the time we returned to the ship and had to use our high beams to locate each other. The helicopter was coughing and gasping for its final bits of nourishment as it settled on the landing pad. The team poured out on deck, crowding around for the news. They had caught up with the deserted *Christina* and were chomping at the bit for revenge. I held up my camera, basking in my moment of glory. "Hey! Everyone should congratulate Pete. He found his balls today. He carried me seven miles into Canadian airspace."

"Give me five, dude." Lee, the impudent little shit, got Pete to slap palms with him. "Way to go, Commander. You'll be hanging with the cool crowd in no time."

In traditional state trooper style, Natalia had found some more bubbly. She sprayed it so directly into our faces, we had no choice but to choke down at least some of it. Not that I cared. I stretched out my tongue for more. After some hesitation, so did Pete.

"How does it feel to be a rule breaker?" asked Josh, slapping Pete on the back. "Was it fun?"

"Oh, his panties were all in a twist, but he got over it," I answered before Pete could say a word. Not that he intended to. He was a little overwhelmed by the attention of the gang and was clearly relieved when we hustled the camera into the ready room and slipped the memory card into the computer. The computer had a sixty-inch flat screen monitor that mounted against the wall, lighting up photographs in magnificent detail. We watched as the crucial shots spread across the screen. At first it was just water, a few scattered islands, and a small, white, rectangle in one corner.

Roy tapped at the keys, cutting away the excess ocean and landscape, bringing the rectangle up close. It was a yacht. Captain Josh scratched at his head and held back a murmur of excitement. "See if you can cut in close enough to find its name and number."

"It might be fuzzy."

It was, at first, but Roy was pretty good at film editing. He cleaned it up enough that we could see the legend painted at the bow. "The Sea Kitten; DL 385". I saw the wheels grinding in the captain's head. He was sure he had his culprit, but he wanted proof.

"Ensign, research the registry of the yacht. I want to know when and where it was purchased, who purchased it, and a list of all the ports it harbored in at. Everything you can find."

"Yes, sir," said Roy.

While Roy was checking the registry, Natalia brought me a plate of food and sat next to me. "You missed dinner."

"Yeah," I said, wolfing down the fat, juicy steak the cook had prepared with very little ceremony. "He likes to do that to me. He's a prick."

"You were the best man for the job."

"That, too." I took another huge bite. Flapping around like a kite off the side of a helicopter gave me an enormous appetite. "Usually, he's the pilot on these scouting missions. He likes to fly. He leaves Pete to navigate the ship. He wanted you to himself."

"He didn't have me to himself. Lee and Roy were right there."

"You didn't start something without me?"

"Of course not. Are you jealous?"

"Grumpy. There's a difference."

"You'll feel better after you've eaten."

To make me feel better, she reached across my shoulders and played with the hair at the back of my neck. "I like that you keep your hair a little long. It suits you."

"I don't like haircuts," I growled, but my grumpy mood was going away.

It had left completely by the time Roy was ready with his report. My stomach was full, and Natalia's hand was still at the back of my neck, stroking my hair. Roy set a print-out on the table. "The yacht is registered to Siberian Hands Inc., an import/export company. It took a little digging, but it's an umbrella company for a group of realtors called B&D—Baranov and Denisovich. It was purchased two years ago from a Chinese multi-millionaire, Lu Chang, according to documents. It has docked into only one American port, San Francisco. Its navigational charts are not available."

"That's our man," said Josh positively. He began strolling energetically up and down the room. "We've got him. We're going to nail him."

"Permission to speak freely," interjected Pete.

Josh stopped in mid-stroll. "Speak."

"Shouldn't we call the Canadian guard? Let them make the arrest? They aren't going to ignore the evidence."

Josh crossed his arms over his chest and glowered, his day-old beard growing thicker. He thundered at the commander beneath fearsome brows. "Do you know what will happen if Denisovich is jailed by Canadian authorities? It will get tied up in courts for five years, and Denisovich will never be handed over to the U.S. Our women will never receive the justice they deserve."

"His men will be turned over for the murders."

"Which we can't tie to Denisovich's hands. Neither Amy nor Natalia were touched by Denisovich. They never even talked to Denisovich. They can't swear they saw him do anything."

"We'll find fingerprints."

Josh resumed pacing. "What if he wore gloves? Did you notice how many footprints were in the hangar? It was like trying to sort out prints in a market stall. The boat will be the same. Too many people coming and going. It will take forever to sort them all out. In the meantime, Denisovich's slippery lawyers will be finding ways to get him extradited to Russia. And they will succeed!"

Pete wrung his hands together. He knew what Josh was proposing and as second officer, he felt it was his duty to persuade the captain into using every legal avenue available. "We can't forcibly bring that yacht back into U.S. territory. Canada will never allow it."

Josh wasn't paying much attention to the commander's protests. He looked out at the black night that even rubbed away the moon's existence under the misting sky. "Canada can have the co-conspirators involved in the buying and selling of slaves. Let those filthy rich degenerates squabble it out with their lawyers and try to keep their names out of the papers. I don't care about them. I want Denisovich and the men who kidnapped our girls and murdered Coast Guard personnel, and I will have them. I *will* have them, Pete. Do you have a problem with this?"

"No, sir," he answered, standing stiffly.

"Relax," said Lee, who never thought much about rank and who now gave Pete a familiar hug around the neck. "He's a member of the gang. He had his christening tonight."

"In subservience," I growled at Lee, even as Roy was crushing the commander into a bear hug. I nodded at Pete, though. "You put your big-boy pants on tonight. Leave them on. They look good on you."

Josh brought out the good stuff—a bottle of Jameson—and poured us each a good, stiff drink. "I want all of you to go to bed and get some rest. The ship will set course with the first daylight. We'll be sailing into Canadian waters, using stealth mode. If we encounter the Canadian guard, we will tell them we are on a secret mission to Seattle. The admiralty will verify it. Pete, you are an honorable commander. If you wish to leave the mission, you can return to Ketchikan by helicopter in the morning. I won't request that you come with us."

"With all due respect, sir," said Pete, appearing far more gregarious than usual, "I'm a member of the gang now."

We all saluted. "Then we are all agreed," continued Josh. "What we don't want is for the yacht to learn we are giving chase, which is why we wait for daylight. They are not in a hurry. They will appear to be just one more luxury craft taking a sight-seeing tour. If they don't see us, we can close in."

We prepared to retire for the night, each person taking care of the tools that fit his skill sets. Pete went back to the pilot's cabin and checked the controls for the evening, lingering over the sensitive instruments long minutes before turning them over to the second lieutenant's safekeeping. Josh gathered his maps and rolled them together, stashing them with a bundle in one corner of the ready room. Roy put the computer to sleep, Lee carried our mugs to the galley, and I picked up the camera and binoculars, wrapping them tenderly before sliding them into their cases. They were my special babies, the best high-powered, high-resolution hand-held instruments on the market. I'm not a standard guy. I don't like standard equipment. These babies had just paid back in gold.

Josh approached me on one side and Natalia on the other. Natalia snuggled up under my arm. "I told the captain we should all share this night together. I think we need it."

"Do you agree, Captain?" I asked, examining his face to see if any extra hairs were popping out. He looked relaxed, almost happy. He had his target. It would take more than the Canadians and the Russian Embassy to keep him away from it.

"I agree." Waving to our other two shapeshifting buddies, we entered the captain's suite together.

LEE

It's not easy controlling your instincts when you're a bear. I learned that in my first month of Coast Guard training. When I hit that icy water, my first instinct was to shapeshift. I don't know how many times McCarthy cut me short. "Lee, all your survivors just swam away from you as fast as they could and two died of a heart attack." He made up his own simulations for the bobbing dummies.

That's how Roy made ensign before I did. It didn't bother me, because I reminded the captain of Darkhorse when he was younger. Yeah, I said it. Darkhorse and Josh have been good buddies since they were cubs, still shuffling around in caves. They worked the same fishing boats together in their teens, signed up for Coast Guard training at the same time. Darkhorse earned his bars more slowly than Josh for the same reason Roy advanced over me.

None of us were really that ambitious to make rank, but we're bears. We liked having a pecking order and challenging it. We liked lording it over each other but it was all for show. Secretly, we loved each other as much as an older brother loves his siblings.

I was hurting that night. We all were. Despite our bravado in front of the crew, our feelings were so scraped and raw, we were all struggling hard to keep from shifting. I was really going to miss McCarthy. He was an excellent man. I had pushed aside the image of his death when I saw the little girl, all trussed up like a pig for the barbecue. Her image, I have never been able to filter out.

There was the bitter question Natalia had asked once during our lovemaking. "How is it animals can be so human, and humans can be such animals?"

Darkhorse took her hand and answered her. "That's why there are shapeshifters. We're here to create balance."

The captain had the largest room. He also had the largest bed. All of us had specially-constructed beds with an extra half-inch of reinforced steel for unconscious sleep-shifts, but his was large enough to fit all five of us comfortably and to withstand the strain if one or two of us accidentally popped out our bear skins. It was reassuring and soothing.

Sweet, funny Natalia. She tucked each one of us in, kissing us lightly on the forehead. I closed my eyes and felt her hover over me. I hadn't let myself think about McCarthy until today, when I saw his beloved cutter. I had shoved him back as far as he would go, thinking only about women, beer, and prey. The boat made his death real. He never would have abandoned the *Christina*. He would never have left her anchored helplessly on a lonely, uncharted beach. His spirit had returned to haunt the *Christina*, crying to take her home. It felt like two red-hot coins were sizzling behind my eyelids.

Natalia smoothed back my hair with cucumber-cool fingertips, dissolving the burning spikes of anguish. We would avenge McCarthy. We would avenge Natalia. We would avenge them all. Josh had promised.

Her breasts brushed up again my bare skin. They were

covered with a thin garment that rustled silkily over her swollen nipples. I remained still, letting myself fall under her spell. She was doing something to me, to us. She was lulling us. She was putting all our bear quarrels to sleep. I breathed her in—wildflowers in the spring, the bright scent of spruce needles, liquid sunlight. I breathed her out and I felt my clan breathing with me. We rode on her sweet, bright, liquid touch.

Her smooth, cool garments slid across me, the curves under the soft folds caressing my skin. The same soothing touch she had used to calm me, she used on Josh, kissing his knotted brow until it smoothed, and softening the lines around his mouth with her fingertips. The silky fabric rustled again. I laid quietly, feeling her movement, feeling her circle around to include us all, the animal part that wished to roar in anger and despair subsiding.

When she returned to me, I was half-asleep, feeling like I had just received a Swedish massage. This time, when she kissed me, her hand moved down to my crotch and curved underneath my balls. I moaned with bliss. Teasingly, it moved upward until it circled the shaft. I held my breath as she stroked it, her hand moving languidly up and down, finding every pleasure point. My Johnson stood at full attention. I was pulsing hot and ready to burst. Straddling my hips, she guided my cock inside her. I didn't have to do a thing. I couldn't do a thing. I was completely at the mercy of that honey sweet triangle grinding and pressing against my own short hairs, her breasts brushing against my chest as she hovered over me. Up and down she glided until, with a final heave, I felt the last bit of tension and agony explode, leaving nothing but a moment of ecstatic pleasure.

None of us really slept. The closeness of each other was better than the closeness of our dreams. Natalia was the kind of babe that brave men longed for on cold, Arctic nights, but she was also a reminder that she, too, could have become a disappearance and a murder. This reminder made us hold her the way she was meant to be held, like a precious jewel.

At the crack of dawn, we heard the engines turning. Even though this was the day we had all waited for, there was something sad about it. I was almost reluctant to see it begin. Once we busted Denisovich, we could all go back to our normal jobs. Natalia would be patrolling the highways of the South/Central coast. We would be patrolling the oceans. There would probably be so much distance between us most of the time, she would forget us. Women married to coast guard men had the same kind of lives as women married to fishermen. Sometimes, they waited for months at a time for their men to come home. Sometimes, the sea claimed their men, and they didn't come home at all. Natalia was a desirable woman. She would want more than we could offer her.

The cook had fixed a whopping breakfast, complete with fat sausages and piles of scrambled eggs. We should have been wolfing it down with gusto, yet nobody had much appetite. I don't think we ate more than a half-pound of sausage each and a dozen eggs. Natalia pecked at her food like a bird. "You're quiet," I said, sitting next to her.

She shrugged and stirred sugar into her coffee. "Everybody's quiet. It's a big, quiet conspiracy."

"The others are quiet, busy. You're quiet, brooding."

She cradled her cheek in one palm while she sipped the coffee. "I received an e-mail from the state troopers. They've begun an undercover investigation into the motorcycle clubs. They thanked me for my service."

"That's good, isn't it?"

"As of today, I'm on unauthorized leave. I was supposed to remain in Ketchikan and take a plane back to Valdez."

"Why didn't you say something while we were there? We

could have left you at the hospital or given you a ride to a hotel."

"I didn't want to. I didn't want to leave any of you." She looked out at the dull, slowly awakening day. "And I want to see this fight to the finish, even if it means losing my job."

"If the Canadians find us, they might impound our vessel."

A roguish smile snaked across her face. "That might be the cherry on top. State trooper dismissed for illegally crossing into Canada in a Coast Guard vessel whose team records from birth to present date are full of redacted files. I checked, if you want to know. The ship has a nice computer. I'm officially a mystery woman. I could even become a vigilante."

She said it dryly enough to sound half-serious. I filled my mouth with toast to stifle my growl. "You couldn't. There wouldn't be enough criminals left over for us."

She chased a piece of egg across her plate, then popped it in her mouth, sighing. "If I had brought my gun… if I always kept my gun on me." A tear trickled down her face. "I wish I was a shape-shifting bear. That would have put them in their place."

"Hey, now." I dabbed at her tears with a paper napkin. Usually, I could get people to lighten up by saying a lot of dumb shit, which came naturally to me anyway, but it clearly wasn't going to work this time. I fumbled around for something to say. "My mom can't shapeshift, but she's still the most kick-ass woman in the village. She rescued two small children from a flood when she was sixteen. The village was so thankful, they gave her a snow machine."

She appeared thankful for the diversion. "How did she meet your dad?"

"That's where it gets interesting." I got up and walked her to the window. The open sea stretched out on one side, a tangle of water and land on the other. We clung to the canopied coastline. It would take at least six hours to close in on the yacht. There wasn't much to do except pass the time getting to know each other, keeping our eyes peeled for snipers. Those bastards were clever. I wouldn't put it past them to send someone out to swing around and keep an eye on things.

I listened to the low mutter of the engines. "Since my mother had a snow machine, she went out with the others who searched for missing people. It happens a lot in remote areas. Kids stray on their way home from school. Somebody runs out of gas on the trail, leaving them stranded. Fishing and hunting accidents. Sudden storms. Anyone with a snow machine joins the search. Usually, they find their missing people and bring them home, although sometimes it's too late."

A diffused sun brightened up the top of her head, where soft curls of hair were making an escape from her barrette. She looked like one of those sea maidens hanging off the bow of a ship. A grown-up Goldilocks. I touched her hair. "This time, they were searching for a hunter. He was twelve hours late coming home, and the wife was getting worried. My mom found him. His leg had been badly mauled by a bear and he was speaking gibberish. They got him back to the village and fixed him up. But they were puzzled. Why didn't the bear kill the hunter?"

"Your dad was the bear?"

"Yes. He was from another village, but he knew things about the bastard. The hunter had married his cousin. He knew the hunter beat his wife and abused his daughter. My dad met him in the woods to confront him about it, to warn him. They got in an argument and the hunter swung around his rifle. Dad said he didn't even think; he just shifted. The hunter was completely petrified. His hair turned white. Dad mauled him but spared his life."

"How did your dad hook up with your mom?"

I laughed. Her eyes were no longer deep and sorrowful. They glittered brightly with interest for my story. "My dad never strayed far from the hunter. He didn't want him to die, just to be nice to his family. When he saw my mom lug that worthless piece of shit up on the snow machine, he decided, right then, that was the girl he wanted to marry. He introduced himself to the village, which had terrible effects on the hunter. Every time he saw my dad walking through the streets, he would start jabbering. After a while, the hunter got the nickname Monster Man because he was the man who saw monsters."

I stroked back her hair, loving the way the strands curled around my fingers. "We are a funny people, Natalia. We jeer at people like the hunter who lose their wits over a shapeshifter; but we all know the truth. The elders know. The shaman always sees right away. When we hold the long dances in the dark night, the shapeshifters always appear. We can't help ourselves. The shadows betray our spirits. My mother knew what he was soon after they started dating, and eventually she learned the whole truth about the hunter, piece by piece. She says it made her love him more."

She rested her cheek against the window, her face so soft and tender, I wanted to kiss her raspberry lips. "What do your parents do now?"

"Mom gives first aid courses. Dad is an electrical technician. Hates the job. He says every time he gets jolted, he changes into a bear. But you can't get him to do anything else."

"My dad's a state trooper," she volunteered. "My mom's a regular housewife. They didn't really like me following in dad's footsteps, but these are modern times. A lot of young people are marrying outside the Russian communities. We're creating new businesses. The Russia we've been clinging to for three hundred years isn't the same motherland. *This* is our motherland now."

The raspberry lips turned upward as she looked into my eyes. "They understand. I don't want to go back. I want my own life."

"You can have your own life," I promised her. "I have land in Galina. I could quit the Coast Guard and join forestry. We could open a mom-and-pop store. You can be whoever you want to be. I'll be there. I'll support you."

Her luscious lips wrapped around mine, giving me a taste of her sweet saliva. It was like nectar. She broke away just as my mouth began opening hers. "You can't do that, Lee. Your team needs you."

"They need Roy. Roy can swim among the ice floes in sub-zero weather. I'm a land animal."

"You love your job."

There was no arguing with that. I liked challenging jobs, jobs that pitted me face to face with Mother Nature's wrath, and the Coast Guard was the most challenging of all. There was more to it, though. I liked search and rescue; I loved being the first line of defense. It was times like these when I was reminded our skills went beyond our ability to fight all obstacles. They were the stealthy hand that cut the fuse on the dynamite. Everything we did from this moment on could prevent or provoke an international incident.

If Natalia understood she was sitting on a disaster waiting to occur, she didn't show it. As the ship sailed deeper into Canadian waters, the crew tensed and readied their weapons. Captain Josh took over the helm.

Josh knew his ship the way a man knows his woman. He was the best navigator in the Arctic and understood the island archipelago like no other. He guided the boat through thin, narrow channels, scarcely causing a ripple on the nearby shores. The engines purred, soft and low, as we slipped along a seascape dotted with secret passages.

Two shots fired into the air, one from an enlisted man's upright rifle and one from across the water. I grabbed Natalia by the arms and pulled her into a crouch. "Stay low. I'm joining the captain."

I didn't need to join him. He was rumbling down the stairs toward me, bent at the waist, his knees jogging in front of him. He pointed to the stern. "Get the others. Let's go. We're shifting."

I slapped once at their doors as I raced toward the metal ladder at the back of the boat. Josh was already halfway down and shifting by the time I reached it. I threw off my clothes and swung over the side, dropping into the water like a torpedo. Three other furry muzzles popped up around me. Another shot fired in our boat's direction. We swam around to the side to have a look at our assailants.

There were two of them, in a streamlined skiff built for speed and very little else. It wasn't a fisherman's practical boat. It was vulnerable to capsizing in choppy water. Josh began swimming in their direction, and we followed. If we got there before they noticed us, we could tip them.

One of the ambushers fired another round. Afraid of attracting the Canadian guard, our ship remained silent. The assailants had started reloading when one tugged at the sleeve of the other and pointed toward us. Instead of firing at us, though, they started their engines. Even with high-powered rifles, they were reluctant to take on four massive bears, one of which was, inexplicably, a polar bear. We began paddling furiously behind them but knew we couldn't catch them, not in a high speed chase.

A whistling noise sped past my ears toward the skiff. There was a "pop," then the engine blew sky-high. Our two attackers rained down in a fury of flaming boards and engine parts. They lay still on the water, face down, arms stretched. I turned toward the boat, looking for whoever was responsible for the shot. Natalia stood on deck, carbine in her hands. She looked smoking hot.

ROY

I don't pretend to know much about women. They play by their own rules and have their own goals. The one thing I do know is, they can twist you up and get you so confused, you find yourself doing things you swore you would never do. You make compromises against your better judgment. You tell them your secrets. Natalia had that effect.

We should have left her in Ketchikan, but instead, we took her with us. Though I couldn't tell the others, I assisted her. I gave her access to the computer and showed her how to open first level files—the kind of files the police and state troopers would read, not the encrypted ones. She may have sent a few phony e-mails to her superiors stating how the team needed her on the case, but if it ever came into question, I hadn't seen a thing.

That was the effect she had on me. It was worse on Josh. He'd given her a gun! He'd let her come with us on a dangerous mission. And now... hot damn. She had fired the gun. Josh remained circling in the water a good ten minutes longer than necessary before climbing up the side into the boat. Slowly and methodically, he retrieved his clothes, inspecting each piece with his mouth downturned before putting it on. Natalia arrived on deck just as he was tucking his shirt into his pants. "You blew up a boat," he said stiffly.

She straightened his collar and brushed at his shoulders. "True. They were getting away."

"You blew up two people."

If she was dismayed about her singular act of violence, she didn't show it. "We couldn't afford to have them informing the cruise ship. Besides, they shot Pete."

I thought he was going to shift again, right on the spot, but he controlled himself. "What? Where?" he sputtered, his face flushing dark, then pale. "How bad?"

"He was lucky. It was a flesh wound. It bit through the flesh of his arm and embedded in the wall. It didn't hit bone, but it tore a muscle."

Josh began pacing, hands behind his back, muttering. "She blew up two people with a military weapon in Canadian waters. How do we explain that? Who teaches her these things?" He stopped in front of me and looked sharply into my face. I trembled with undefined guilt. "Did you teach her? Are you the reason she does what she pleases?"

"I probably am, sir," I admitted, feeling it was better to agree than to contradict him.

He stood woefully in the middle of the floor, his hands still behind his back. "I suspected as much. You never can trust a Viking with a Russian woman. Now, how do we explain this to the authorities?"

"Let the admiral sort it out," Natalia suggested. "You were fired upon while investigating the murder of McCarthy and his team."

"In a high-speed chase," I added.

"That's how it happened," confirmed Josh. "We were fired

upon and… and one of the enlisted personnel fired back. It was self-defense."

I was growing more confident about our story by the minute. "We had been chasing them so long, we didn't realize we had crossed the border. It was an honest mistake."

"Except, who fired the shot?"

I scratched my chin thoughtfully. "Maybe Pete's willing to take the credit."

"After he was shot?"

I clicked my teeth together. "Tough guy, Pete is. A real hero. After getting shot, he was so angry to see these murderers getting away, he shot back at them. Never meant to hit the fuel tank. That's what happens when both arms aren't fully operational."

"That's a fact, isn't it? Pete was very brave. He'll probably get a medal."

Satisfied that his bases were still covered, he bounded into the pilot's cabin, going up the stairs two steps at a time. Pete was being treated for his wound. He looked pale, but was already gaining the goofy look of someone high on drugs. "Hey, Captain," he croaked cheerfully. "I took one for the team."

Josh patted the uninjured shoulder. "I see you did. You're a good man. I'm going to get you off this boat as soon as I can. Go below, Commander. Check into the infirmary. We'll reach our target area in twenty minutes."

"Permission to remain here," he said in a loopy voice.

"Permission denied. I'll call you in two hours. Get some rest."

Captain Josh regained the wheel, easing the ship in even closer to the island banks, sliding around bends with the engines murmuring so low, they sounded like cats purring. It was a miracle nobody was close enough to hear the shots or see the explosion. Again, maybe not. The islands were largely deserted this time of year. The tourist season was over. Fishermen were throwing their nets into the icy waters of the northern Pacific. The small towns sleepily curled around themselves, waiting for spring.

Once the bodies were discovered, it wouldn't be hard to defend our case, not with the deserted cutter so close to the scene. It would just be difficult to explain ourselves if we got caught snooping around Vancouver. It was Captain Josh's expertise that we all depended on to keep that from happening.

We reached the target area in the length of time the captain said we would. He settled the ship back into a little cove and dropped anchor. It was a good location. The cove curved inland enough to form a natural barrier, yet left a wide mouth at one end that allowed us an unrestricted view of the ocean from our swampy port of overhanging trees and tangled brush. In our hiding place, so close to the shore, the boat rocked against a bed of surfacing seaweed, and we could see the white dot of the cruise ship six miles away. We aimed the telescopic lens on the pilot's deck at it and took turns watching the fuzzy panorama of activity.

We spent about an hour studying the layout and watching visitors arrive. We found no sign of the Canadian Coast Guard, and few indicators of activity apart from the cruise ship. Some of the visitors came in by boat, buzzing up to the stern and using the ladders, some came by helicopter. We recognized a few faces from the Internet news feed. Arrogant and wealthy, they strutted around with their air of diplomatic immunity, flickering in and out of the telescopic lens.

After giving him his two-hour rest, Pete was summoned from sickbay. He arrived still a little fuzzy-headed, but it was nothing two cups of the cook's stout, black coffee wouldn't fix. Josh gave him an intense look. "Are you with us, Commander?"

"Aye, sir." Pete looked at his surroundings drowsily, his eyes slowly taking in the cul-de-sac the captain had snuggled us into, and the telescope lens fixed at a white spot on the ocean.

"We've got our enemy in the line of sight. My team is headed out. I want you and everyone else to sit tight. That includes Natalia. Make no noise, fire no weapons, do nothing at all once we're out there, no matter what you see."

"Yes, sir," said Pete, looking anxiously at Natalia, while she tapped her foot and pressed her lips together.

Josh stopped in his instructions long enough to glower at Natalia before resuming his speech. "Tell the crew to keep their eyes peeled, Commander, for any extra signs of activity. If we aren't back before the first Canadian guard appears, raise anchor and hightail it out of here. Get back into U.S. waters. And take this woman with you. If she kicks and screams, tie her up and lock her in her quarters."

"Captain, we would be leaving you stranded."

He huffed. "If you're caught in these waters without so much as permission from the port authorities, there will be such a stink about U.S. trespassing and spying, it will take a hundred years to air it all out." With a self-satisfied sigh, he added, "There is no jurisdiction for bears."

The atmosphere in the cabin was rather glum. None of the human crew was happy about being left out of the main flurry, but there was no choice. The law can only be bent so far before it breaks. We'd always been on good terms with Canada. Canadians were reasonable people and as eager as anyone to put the bad guys away, but they couldn't turn their heads at the unthinkable, when the unthinkable was carnage caused by humans.

The captain led us into the ready room and closed the door gently. The privacy was meant to spare the rest more pain at being excluded from the final stage of our pursuit. He gathered us into a huddle like football players, pumping us up, allowing us to taste our own adrenaline.

"When we hit the deck, I want you fierce. I want you to be the most terrifying thing they've ever encountered. I want them to be so terrified, they drop their drawers and shit, but remember: We don't care about the buyers. Law enforcement will take care of them. All we care about are Denisovich and his men. We get them, and we get out."

"How do we know law enforcement will come?" asked Lee, his mind still going over the miles of unpatrolled waters.

"Believe me, Lee. If you're doing your huffing, puffing best, somebody's going to sound an alarm. They aren't going to stand around with a dozen shredded bodies and wait for someone to show up."

"And the girls, boss? What about the girls?"

"We'll stay close by until we hear someone. The girls will be all right, Lee. I'll notify the admiralty as soon as we're back with the *Ursa*. Nobody wants an international incident; not Canada, not Russia, not us."

It's not very difficult to be terrifying when you're twelve feet tall and weigh two thousand pounds. I was a little shorter than Josh when I was in bear form and had a narrower head, but these small differences didn't register in the mind of someone faced with a roaring animal towering over them. Terrified people freeze. They panic. They do stupid things. And they would be scrambling like rats to get off a sinking ship.

The anticipation of putting the fear of the almighty in some of these black-hearted scoundrels had me pumping so hard, I was shaking. I kicked off my shoes and unbuckled my pants. Natalia breezed over with her forever scent of wildflowers and slipped her hands inside the loose trousers, squeezing my buttocks. She pulled me close, so my chest rubbed against her. "Come back safe. I want all my men."

I kissed her, exploring with my tongue and would have done a little exploring of my own inside her pants, but Josh pulled us apart. "Natalia," he said sternly, gripping her arm. "I need you to promise me. You will not intervene."

"I won't intervene," she said, looking up at him innocently. "I'm just giving each of you my personal blessing." She snuggled up to him to prove it.

He took her arms and held her back. "You will stay on the boat. If the boat leaves, you will leave on the boat. Promise me."

"I'll stay on the boat," she echoed, making a face. "I promise."

Notably, he still buttonholed Pete as we filed out. "Hold her to her word."

"Yes, sir," said Pete.

As naked humans, we climbed over the guardrail and down the ladder. As bears, we slipped into the water. It was the warmest ocean I had ever been in while in bear form. It felt strange; as though I had just landed in the tropics. I swam languidly. I knew the others weren't as comfortable in the wide, open sea as I was, and I didn't want to look like I was showing off in front of them. Darkhorse and Lee were the most unhappy. They held their heads up stiffly, dogpaddling. Josh was an islander. He was farther south than usual, but these were still islands. He swam confidently, almost keeping up with me.

The yacht had a metal ladder to one side of the stern. Josh led the way, with Darkhorse right behind him. He paused and peered over the edge. Beckoning to us, he scurried onto the deck and ducked behind the stairs leading to the next level. When it came my turn, I halted. Someone was crossing the floor. I held my breath as muffled steps strolled to the far end guardrail and a man looked over the bow. After lighting a cigarette and taking a few drags, he tossed it overboard and returned to the main party.

Quickly, I slipped over the edge and joined the team with Lee at my tail. Josh indicated in bear sign that we were each to go in a separate direction. My way led me through a service door left partially open. I calculated the number of steps I needed to reach the door several feet to the right of the stairs, in an exposed area. A shadowy figure flicked by at the far end, then a moment of unbroken silence passed. Staying close to the wall, I walked rapidly to the open door and slipped inside.

The lighting was poor. Only a single bulb lit a hallway with pantry shelves on either side. Ahead were the sizzling pots and the clangs of a kitchen. I wandered into a galley filled with thick cooking smells, remaining in the shadows and crouching behind counters and stoves.

The cooks bustled in and out the swinging doors, attending the guests in the dining room. Through the swinging doors, I saw little glimpses of that other world, a world of chandeliers, crystal, tall windows and plush seats. When it swung in the other direction, there was this: an overcrowded space teeming with overflowing dishwater, bubbling oil, grease-splattered floors, smoke and steam.

As I became accustomed to the dim lighting, the crowded conditions and the confusion, my attention was caught by something that seemed to be completely apart and separate from the rest of the dining preparations. A thick brocade curtain partitioned off the entrance to another room in the farthest, darkest corner of the kitchen. One gentleman, in full chef's uniform, went in and out, bringing delicacies inside and returning with empty dishes. Only one chef—the others pretended he didn't exist.

This kindled my curiosity. With all the discretion that can be squeezed into two thousand pounds of fur balls, I slithered under a table and inched my way up to the doorway. Daringly, my heart pounding, I slipped through it.

I don't know what I expected at a slave trade, but I didn't expect this. I was visualizing the girls chained up in cages in the cargo area, not passed out in a room lavishly furnished in scarlet and gold. A huge matching set of settees, armchairs, cushions, and daybeds were scattered around, and complemented by ornate, round tables. There was champagne, chocolates, and finger foods laid out on the little tables and a handful of upper-crust male citizenry with silk suits that would feed the homeless for a month and jeweled rings that would put your eyes out. These elite, well-heeled gentleman stopped at a table now and then to eat a cracker with stuffed crab or a chocolate-covered strawberry and look over the merchandise.

The merchandise was the twelve girls. They were all nude. They all seemed sound asleep as they were poked and prodded, yet never once stirred. They also appeared to have been arranged in their positions. Some were sitting up, their heads lolling against the back of their settee, one leg stretched in front, another on the floor. Some were stretched out with an arm over their heads, legs thrown in wide abandonment.

They barely moaned when a prospective buyer lifted their arms to smell underneath, felt their breasts and their velvety little snatches, then turned them over to examine their bottoms. There was something sickening, unreal, and totally macabre in the way they would dispassionately run their hands down the soft, unresponsive bodies, as though examining prize livestock. My stomach churned and I felt a bitter, burning taste in my mouth as I watched in horror and agony, unable to look away, unable to prevent these young girls from being violated until I received the signal.

A thirtyish young man with a long face and cruel ferret

eyes wriggled his fingers inside the newly-blossoming triangle of a girl who was arranged on a sofa with her head resting on her arm, one leg bent at the knee and propped on the couch, the other dangling. "Too loose," he announced. He had a high, nasal voice. He sniffed his fingers. "Doesn't smell that good, either."

I heard someone laugh. "Pick another." The voice had a thick Russian accent. I swung my head in the speaker's direction. It was one of Denisovich's men. I felt a lightning bolt hit my brain and I rumbled deep in my chest. I was supposed to wait. We were all supposed to stay quiet until Josh found Denisovich, no matter what the situation. With each passing minute, the bile boiling up inside became more bitter, the sheer magnitude of what these men had done more unbearable, the rage rumbling like a volcano.

"How's this one?" asked the author of my blazing torments. He pulled up a young, half-Native girl by her limp arms from off a chair. Oddly, she had been placed in the least compromising position, barely noticeable among the blatant display of village girl treasures. Her skin was light as snow, her hair slick and black. She looked like a child, no more than fifteen. "Nobody's laid a hand on her," he said, picking her up and spreading her out on a roomy daybed. He smoothed the hair away from her face, set her arms by her side and opened her legs to expose a silky triangle of black hairs that had barely begun to sprout. "We think she could be a virgin."

Mr. Prick for a Nose ran a hand up the inside of her thighs. "Tight as a drum."

"Don't break it. She's our main attraction."

"How do I know she's not a druggie?"

"No, no. They've been on drugs only two days to keep them compliant. We were clean about it. No drugs. No sex with them. Just make them ready for the market."

The hackles on my back were standing up like porcupine quills. I felt if I had to hold back any longer, I was going to explode. Just when I was about to let loose, signal be damned, somebody screamed; if you could call it that. It was a horrible, shattering sound, two pitches higher than a normal man's voice, followed by a long, sobbing, pleading wail. That was the signal.

I reared up on my hindlegs, the guard hairs shooting down my back like spikes, the great scruff around my neck bristling with fury, my lips curled back in a savage snarl. I roared. For one moment, all activity was suspended. Even the drugged girls opened their heavy-lidded eyes in wonder. The chef, who had been clearing clutter made from wine glasses and plates, pissed his pants. My vile, hated, sworn enemy fumbled for his sidearm, three seconds too late. I squeezed his shoulders with my front paws and opened my mouth, letting him get a good whiff of my hot, wild breath, then closed my jaws slowly over his neck and squeezed. I wanted him to understand, in his final seconds, what it was like to be meat.

The degenerate business tycoons were pressing as close to the wall as they could get. If it had been a possibility, they would have pressed right into it. Mr. Prick Nose was still leaning against the daybed but had sunk to his knees. The captain's instructions drummed dimly in the back of my mind. We were only to take out Denisovich and his men. We were to leave the mucky-muck's to the higher-ups. I just couldn't make myself care enough to listen. I gave Mr. Stinky Fingers one long slash across the face with four razor-sharp claws. He might live through it. Some people did, but they never forgot what happened.

I trotted back to the service door and looked out toward the main deck. It was gloriously splendid. Absolute mayhem. The rest of the team had already polished off the crew. The panicked guests didn't have the wits to do anything except scramble for shelter and cower. We were to terrify them. Remaining on my hind legs, I thundered out, my bass voice ricocheting across the stairway.

I must have been their worst nightmare: a solid white bear with splashes of blood running from his throat to his stomach, standing up to his full height, like a twelve-foot heavyweight boxer in a fur coat. Nobody moved. Nobody lifted a finger. There were a few slobbering sounds, and I believe someone was praying. My voice boomed out in an air-shattering roar and the three bears behind me stood up on their hind legs, with the captain topping my size by two inches. His enormous shoulders swelled under the great hump on his back. His black lips wrinkled away from a double row of serrated, carnivorous teeth, meeting with a massive jaw. He was primal. His race was ancient. It soared through the flashing black eyes. His roar was a roll of thunder, answered by the others as a background chorus. It echoed through the yacht, already shuddering with the horrors of its new-found ghosts and mingled with the natural sounds of the ocean's wildlife.

Just as the captain had predicted, somebody, either unwittingly or willfully, shot a flare. If they were unwitting, they shot it because they thought it was a gun. If it was willful, they probably reasoned it was better to face the Canadian guard than four bears. Whatever the reason, it was a good time to make an exit. We jumped over the rail and hit the water simultaneously.

Eventually, someone did find a gun. A few shots rang out, but by then we were a half-mile away from the yacht. No little girls went tumbling over the side of the boat, so it was a safe bet the congregation of spineless human refuse were not about to compound the problems they were already facing by adding murder charges. We paddled noiselessly in smooth, clean V's, only our heads showing above the water. From the distance, we could be any marine animal. We swam silently, putting as much ocean as we could between ourselves and the yacht before the Coast Guard came.

We heard the first helicopter just as the island was coming into clear view. Another clattered in, its propellers shrieking, engines whining, rumbling through the air. I turned my head to look back. The yacht was no more than a tiny toy bobbing on the ocean, with two tiny choppers hovering overhead. Streaming toward it were three tiny boats, all so small, they looked like a swarm of gnats. The captain nudged me, and I turned purposely back toward shore.

I could tell by the warm current that we were going into shallower water. The captain veered toward a small depression in the outward swing of the rocky strip of land and entered our hidden cove. The *Ursa* was nowhere to be found. We had hoped they would leave, but had not really expected them to. A small suspicion had lurked that they would defy us because Natalia was involved, and that was what she did. Josh snorted in what could only be interpreted as relief. The boat probably lit out with the first sound of chopper blades. Those were Pete's instructions. I wondered how well he was keeping Natalia at bay.

I felt my feet claw at a sandy bottom that gradually rose until I was padding through seven inches of water to a thin strip of beach. I ambled through the brush unhurriedly, listening to the soft snuffle of the others shouldering their way through the forest matting. Once we were in the dense woods, we sat down for a little rest and bear talk.

Lee chuckled low in his chest. "Did you see that? We turned their hair gray. One guy pooped in his pants."

I rolled back on the velvety moss. "Did you get him, Captain? Did you get Denisovich?"

Josh was scratching his back blissfully against a tree. "I did."

"You bet he did," confirmed Darkhorse enthusiastically. "Denisovich tried to get away. He was hanging out around the swimming pool, sitting in a deck chair, soaking that fat gut with sunshine. A couple of his crew were there, some guests and their sun bunnies. He had a girl oiling his skin.

"When he saw the captain, he grabbed her and tried to shove her in front of him in a bear offering. The poor girl was so terrified, she stumbled and fell to the floor, but Josh just ignored her. He walked right past her, showing his teeth and growling. Fat Gut jumped into the pool! Maybe he thought Josh wouldn't go after him in the water. It was quite a show. Did you drown him or fillet him to death, Josh?"

"A little of both," said Josh, satisfying his itch with a sigh. "If Pete followed my instructions to the letter, we have a journey ahead of us. I told him not to stop until he was back in U.S. territory. We'll be mostly on land. I know all the shallowest crossings. If we remain in bear form, we should be back in Ketchikan within three days."

It was a good thing it was early winter and not midsummer, or the heat in this southern region would be unbearable while wrapped in a polar bear skin. I stuck to the darkest, densest parts of the woods, which was a good strategy for another reason besides staying cool. The islands were full of brown bears, but from an aerial view, a white bear would stand out like a sore thumb.

We were making good time. One thing about the Panhandle islands, their length consistently ran north to south and their width was always narrow. They chained together so tightly that many of them were a shallow, easy crossing. We were also getting hungry. We had crossed two islands and were halfway through a third when we burst into a clearing covered with blueberry bushes. Josh sighed and sat on his haunches. "Time to eat, ladies."

I should have been starving. At first, I shoveled the berries in, but the sight of the girls wouldn't leave me. I understood now how Lee must have felt when he saw the girl tied to the bed. The hopelessness of being unable to protect her. Seeing her horror. The blueberries no longer tasted so sweet and I dawdled, picking at them with disinterest.

Josh waddled over next to me and grunted as he squatted on the ground. "Something on your mind?" he asked.

I scratched at my nose so he wouldn't see the wet fur. "I saw the girls, Captain. They were all drugged up and put out on display without a stitch of clothes on. These rat bastards were putting their nasty hands all over them. Pretty village girls, some really young. I wanted to kill them all—the rat bastards, I mean, not the girls."

"It's good they were asleep," growled Josh. "They won't remember it. They're safe now. They're being rescued. You did your job well, Roy. C'mon. We've got to haul ass a few more islands to make it to Ketchikan."

The territory was becoming familiar. As we crossed one stream that veined out from the channel, we saw the bits of wreckage from the exploded speed boats, and a few body parts caught up in overhanging brush. We were coming up on the deserted *Christina*. We sped across the island, lifting our snouts and flaring our nostrils to track her. She wasn't alone. Clamoring over a hill, we looked down at where she was docked. Anchored beside her, bobbing in the water, was the *Ursa*.

Had Josh not been in bear form for an entire day, he probably would have popped into it now, but he had spent all his juice on swimming, fighting, and cross-country travel. He took human form before the raft they sent for us arrived. Josh put on his clothes without a word, climbed into the raft and floated to the boat with his arms over his chest, then tramped up the stairs to the pilot's cabin two steps at a time. "I thought I told you not to stop until we reached Alaskan waters," he barked.

"Yes, sir," said Pete, holding up his hand in a painful salute.

"Then who gave the order for you to stop here?"

Natalia handed Josh a cup of coffee. "I did."

He was eager for the hot brew but sputtered. "You did? You can't give orders to a military officer. You're civilian personnel."

"And a state trooper investigating a civilian crime committed on Alaskan soil."

"We already talked with a Canadian vessel," said Pete, coming between the two before they had a real chance to quarrel and Josh had to go through another cooling-off period. "We are here to retrieve our vessel by order of the Alaskan governor."

"You told them that?"

Pete hedged a little, then straightened and looked Josh in the eye. "I was telling them that when they received another call. I guess it was more important. They told Natalia she could check for signs of criminal activity, then left."

"You lucky son-of-a-bitch."

We decided to pull the *Christina* out while we had a chance. The men that had spearheaded the operation were all dead. The *Christina*, sitting in Canadian waters, would just complicate things. The dead snipers, blown to bits by our own Miss True Heart, were just a complication of Kidnapping Gone Wrong. Let the Canadians sort it out.

It was an unusually clear evening. The stars and moon gave off so much sparkling radiance, we scarcely needed our lights. We had all moved out to the main deck, propping folding chairs close to the guardrails so we could sprawl back and listen to the constant murmur of the ocean. A large cooler full of beer sat between us. The boat chugged gently, pulling the ghostly cutter behind it. It felt like a funeral procession.

"McCarthy was a good man," said Josh, waving around a beer bottle. "He was one of the first advocates for special shapeshifting units." He poured his drink over the side. "Drink up, McCarthy."

"McCarthy even tried to create a unit for beavers," chuckled Darkhorse with that husky voice people use when digging through memories. "They make damned good construction workers, but they weren't the best at search and rescue. They drowned more dummies than they rescued."

"Beaver shapeshifters don't do well at Arctic operations," I said. "We had to rescue a few who were chasing down a pipeline saboteur. They were lost and suffering from hypothermia."

"Here's to McCarthy," said Darkhorse. "His heart was always in the right place." He leaned over the rail and watched as the liquid streamed from the bottle and into the ocean. "We got them, old man. The rat-sucking, girl-thieving, back-stabbing bastards. We got them. Rest in peace."

I stood up just a little drunkenly and waved my bottle toward the rail. "McCarthy, may the Valkyries carry you on wings to the place where only the brave and noble of heart are allowed to enter. May you endure the kisses of a thousand beautiful women." I poured my bottle over the rail and nearly toppled over with it. Natalia caught me, pulling me back.

"All right, Eric the Red. Come back to earth now. We all love you, even when you put on your war helmet." She gave me a kiss to prove it and made me sit back down. She remained standing, propped against the railing. "I never met McCarthy, but he was a member of our finest military force and a friend to everyone on this team. That's good enough for me. Captain McCarthy, this is in your honor." She poured out her beer.

Lee had been unusually quiet. He sat back in his chair, a dark scowl on his face. I knew he'd looked up to McCarthy, but I didn't think the attachment had been that strong.

"I killed the lieutenant," he blurted. We all turned to him in wordless surprise. "I killed the man who sold him out. The one who led Denisovich to McCarthy's house." He stood up and yelled toward the *Christina*, "Did you hear that, Captain? I saw the lieutenant on the yacht, and I killed him. I killed the traitor." He raised his beer high, then dumped it.

Josh tried very hard not to appear perturbed and finally managed. "I think McCarthy should be drunk enough by now."

Lee threw himself back in his chair and popped open another bottle. "I damned sure hope so. We need some for us."

The lights of Ketchikan were twinkling in the distance. I closed my eyes and relaxed in the cool northern air. It was good to be home.

What? Not a single embrace? Not one person thanking me for saving them two days off their savage ramble through the wilderness? I suppose I should get used to it. Their instinct was to grumble. They would grumble if Gordon Ramsay invited them to dinner. I think Josh was relieved at the chance to grab the *Christina* without having to jump through a lot of diplomatic loops, but he certainly didn't want to show it. He pulled the whole military/civilian rank on me, but it worked both ways. As a civilian law officer, I wasn't obligated to take his orders.

I didn't really have to strong-arm Pete. I knew the cap would be easier on him, though, if he thought I was the culprit. Pete didn't want to leave without the team, either. As soon as we were within range of the abandoned cutter, it was easy to convince him to wait for them there. We had a good cover story, and the Canadians didn't want a quarrel with us any more than we wanted one with them. He's not used to gambling but he was able to drum up a good poker face, probably from all those years of following the chain of command.

Pete's an all right dude. He doesn't look half-bad, with short-cropped hair leaning more toward brown than blonde, hazel eyes—which, contrary to opinion, did not reflect his emotions. They were always murky, unless he was wearing blue. Then, they looked like the ocean on a clear day. He was stacked, too. Not off-the-chart powerhouse stacked like my four hunks in furs, but enough to show nice muscular definition under his Coast Guard button-up. He'd make a good catch for any single girl without a lengthy waiting list, just not me. The chemistry wasn't there. He didn't have the pizzazz. The shapeshifters did.

It's hard to think clearly when I think about my boys. Sometimes, I find it hard to separate them—except Roy, who looked like he stepped off a nineteenth-century Norwegian whaling ship. He didn't think quite the same as the others. He didn't have their competitive streak. Often, I felt like he was holding his abilities back and channeling them into his hobbies. Yet they respected him as though he was a senior officer instead of an ensign. Darkhorse told me that Lee once broke the ice away from a tugboat by himself and manually pulled the boat into an ice-free zone. The pilot was so amazed, all he could do was get down on his knees and bless Iliamna, the goddess who rules the Bristol Bay, for sending her angels. He didn't see Roy as a bear, but a vision of white light. I've seen him shift. He doesn't look like an angel of light—he looks like a mountain of fur, claws, and teeth.

When they are human, they are just like any Arctic seafaring men I've ever known. Their eyes are always fastened to the far north with its black winter storms. They spend months living right on the edge of death. When they come to port, they love music and dancing. They love their women and treat them like queens, even the women who don't stay true to them while they are gone. It's the wild seas that call them. It's their loneliness that tames them.

Just like seamen, they get grumpy, but they are the only seamen I know that literally turn into bears. It's okay with me if they tear off their clothes and jump into a pool of water whenever they get mad, but I didn't want them to think, even once, they could use their bear faces to intimidate me. And I thought they should be at least a little happy to see me. Instead, they were grouchy as, well, bears.

Their faces glowered while they supervised the crew preparing the winch to haul out the *Christina*. They didn't like the way the boat was being handled and hooked up the winch themselves, easing the cable by hand until they got her into deep water. Then, in a black funk, they dragged out a cooler full of beer, flopped down in some chairs, and began to drink themselves silly.

What's a gal gotta do to keep her northmen happy? I complained to Pete. As my co-conspirator, I kept him in my confidence. He was the one person who could teach me about living around shapeshifters. I had no question I was going to live with them. For me, it was just a matter of figuring out how. Now that we were in Alaskan waters, Pete had a peaceful expression on his face. He remained at the wheel, his eyes fixed on the spotted seascape sliding by the windows, and didn't answer right away.

"I see the antacids worked," I quipped dryly.

"What? I'm sorry. It wasn't that apparent, was it? The ulcers?"

"I've got a dad."

"Yeah." We cleared the last of the chain and churned out into open water. He turned the controls over to the second lieutenant and walked with me into the galley. "When they shift into bears, all their instincts are the instincts of a bear. They know they are human in bear form, but the longer they stay bears, the harder it is for them to remember the difference. They remained bears a very long time. They are trying to become human again."

He poured some of the cook's brutal coffee and added sugar to make it more palatable. "There is a story of the first woman to tame a shapeshifting bear."

"Didn't she trick him during a spirit dance?"

"No. Spirit dances are sacred, but in ancient days, shapeshifters weren't always reliable. Sometimes, when they shifted, they would return to the wild and forget about their human part, especially if they were young. This happened to a young man the first time he shapeshifted at a dance. He ran into the forest and didn't return. They searched for months before giving up on him."

"The girl found him?"

"Don't spoil my story. I heard this straight from a Native American elder." He adjusted his wounded arm, either for sympathy or because it really was uncomfortable. Maybe a little of both. He had been stalwart. "The village forgot about the young man. It had been three years since his disappearance. One day, a family was traveling across the tundra when they were faced with a sudden storm. The storm was so thick and furious, they couldn't see two feet ahead of them. They huddled together to ride it out, but when the sky cleared, they discovered they were missing their sixteen-year-old daughter. All that could be seen for miles around was an unbroken blanket of snow."

I had heard, throughout my life, at least a dozen stories about shapeshifters, but they'd all had an urban legend quality to them—until now. Now, the stories all seemed to be true, except a few that had been warped and twisted for scaring children into behaving. According to Roy, there are a lot of things we should believe but don't, and a lot we shouldn't believe, but do.

I watched the team through the galley windows. Their

expressions were softening; their brows weren't so heavy. In full human form, Lee and Darkhorse didn't even have beards, and very little body hair. Their skin was like velvet. Right now, though, they looked like hairy mountain men. I turned my attention back to Pete. "So, he found the girl."

He leaned across the table, tapping his finger at my coffee cup. "My story has a point. You should listen closely." He cleared his throat, as though teaching in a classroom. "The parents searched a long time for the girl, then went to the nearest village for help."

"The same one that had lost a young man."

"Yes. The girl was lost and alone in the tundra. She called on the caribou for help, but the caribou ran away. She called on the raven, who took the tiny red ball of the setting sun and handed it to her. She put it in her mouth and ate it just as the new sun was coming up. The red sun in her stomach attracted the shapeshifting bear. At first, she thought he would kill her and was terribly frightened, but he picked her up and carried her to the edge of the forest. There, he changed back into a human for the first time in three years and guided her to his village."

Pete took a final sip of coffee, deciding his break was over. "The legend is, the tiny red ball in her stomach tamed him. From that day forward, there were those who were able to summon the shapeshifting bears and keep them human when they started to go wild because they carry a piece of that tiny red sun. The team believes you carry a piece of that sun."

I gave a short laugh that sounded quirky to my ears. "You don't have to believe it," he said, returning to the pilot's cabin. "The thing is, they do."

I wasn't sure how I was supposed to take his story. The whole idea of a tiny red sun glowing inside my belly that only shapeshifting bears could see was ridiculous. But what wasn't ridiculous was how I felt for them, and how they felt for me. Maybe it was some sort of strange magic, and maybe I should take advantage of it. It was silly not to go out into the nice weather. The guys didn't look grumpy anymore. Just sad. I leaned over Josh and ran my fingers through his hair. It was dark brown and thick. When I buried my hands in it, it sprang up between my fingers like the lush hair of a fur-bearing animal.

"Is it about McCarthy?" I asked, and he nodded. I cradled his head close, swaying thoughtfully with the ship. "We should hold a proper wake."

"We should, shouldn't we?" He gave me what felt more like a thank you kiss than anything else and pulled up another chair for me. I settled in for the duration. It may sound strange coming from a transplanted Russian, but I know plenty about wakes. With so many Irish taking ground-pounder jobs, they've just about become a state trooper tradition.

It was a proper wake. My boys became men again, grieving a fallen comrade. They emptied themselves in human form and not in raging bearskins. I was sorry and sad for them. I let them all know how much I felt their pain, raw and purely human.

In the mid-evening, a draft sprang up and we huddled inside blankets. The lights of Ketchikan twinkled in the distance. "We're home," I said. I think my voice sounded a little deflated. "What do we do now?"

"Make our reports," said Darkhorse sourly.

I raised my voice. "About us? All of us?" If there was a little piece of red sun inside me, I hoped it was shining as bright as a police siren.

Darkhorse tightened the hand he had placed around my shoulders. "There will be a de-briefing. That will take a few days."

"And then?"

"We live on a boat. I don't know where to keep a mama bear. We've never had one before."

None of them knew what to do. Even when we retired to the captain's room and sprawled on the bed, trying to regain some sobriety, none came up with brilliant suggestions that did not involve giving up their careers. That wasn't something I could accept. Even if they didn't love their jobs so much, the public needed them. I couldn't be that selfish.

Clearly, I was supposed to be the one to come up with a master plan. Other women worked things out with their sea-faring men. I'd think of something. In the meantime, there were a lot of other things to keep us busy. The slave-trader yacht was all over the news. The Canadian guard was at a loss to explain why four bears killed an entire crew, but not the guests. They were reluctant to tell the public what the guests were doing on the yacht, but already rumors were flying. The people of Ketchikan knew the answer. It's not something you can keep secret long when the town is that small.

It was a solemn ceremony when we first anchored into the dock. The harbor master and a handful of Coast Guard personnel lined up along the pier, caps tucked under their arms, hands raised in a uniform salute for the pirated *Christina* and her murdered officers. Once we hit solid ground, people were dancing in the streets. They jostled each other to shake our hands. Every bar was open to us for free drinks. We were heroes, at least for that night, and we made the most of it. We drank. We danced on the tables. We sang as we weaved through the streets, supported by each other's arms.

The next day was a different story. Josh gathered us all in the ready room and gave us a sour face—although it was one that wasn't overly grumpy, just hung over. "The admiral is having a hissy fit, or the governor is having a hissy fit and passing it on to the admiral. They are disturbed by a couple of small items in the report. One of the guests was attacked and almost died. He's currently in an induced coma. Can anyone explain this?"

"I might have injured a guest," said Roy, raising his hand.

"Would you care to tell me why?"

"I think he was going for a gun."

"There was only one gun in the room."

"He was going for that gun, after the Russian dropped it."

"I see." Josh's brow furrowed a little and thickened. It must be tough to be the rule-breaking captain of a team of rule-breakers. At some point, it's no longer about chain of command, but just a lot of free-thinking agents. "The admiral is concerned that a member of the Alaskan Coast Guard was killed by a bear. He wished to remind me; military personnel are to be brought in to face trial. Was the lieutenant going for his gun?"

"No, sir," said Lee with a military snap to his voice. "He wasn't quick enough."

"But he had a gun?"

"He had a gun, sir."

"He probably would have gone for his gun if he had been quick enough."

"I expect he would have if he had thought quick enough, but it wouldn't have done much good."

"Both men had probable cause," Josh said cheerily. "Dark-horse, work on Lee a bit. Make him"—he waved his hand around in the air as though the words would appear there—"Governor acceptable."

The state troopers were still up in the air about me. I had been working on their clock, without their authorization once I had received the opportunity to return to Valdez and turned it down, but I had helped solve the biggest missing persons case of the year. The state troopers didn't mind bending rules either, when it brought results. I wondered now how many had met up with shapeshifters; and even, how many were those strange between-world characters.

Our issues were minor and quickly resolved through a few secret phone calls. Canada wasn't as lucky. It had far more to explain to the public than a mysterious attack by bears. When the helicopters first hovered over the yacht and saw the blood-stained deck, they knew this was going to be a tough one. They had rappelled down in full riot gear, expecting enemy fire. All they saw, beyond the scattered dead, was a group of wealthy, well-connected, international businessmen. Extremely terrified businessmen. Some of them drooled and spoke gibberish.

If one perplexing question wasn't enough, another came into view after a search of the vessel. Why were twelve naked young girls crashed out on drugs in one room? The survivors were too far in shock to answer. They were evacuated from the boat and taken into Vancouver for processing.

Once the girls had come out of their drugged state enough to give their names and where they were from, the worst question of them all was put to the businessmen. Why were all the girls on Alaska's missing person's list? Within twenty-four hours, lawyers, diplomats and journalists were popping up in Vancouver like roaches.

Canada got the collar, the glory, and the nightmare of closing the book on an international crime ring. Alaska got its girls. We got our revenge. The bear question was shelved for the more serious ones of criminal proceedings. There wasn't much you could proceed against with bears. It's not exactly like you can pull them from a line-up and state positively, "That's the one." You can't make laws for them. Canadian Parks responded by putting up 'beware of bear' signs and even placing brochures in the harbor master's office. This satisfied the public.

The Canadians were anxious to send the girls home quickly. They even encouraged the Alaska Coast Guard fleet to come get them. I think they were afraid Seattle would swoop in on the girls first and create a big sensation in the city. The Coast Guard responded by sending two helicopters into Vancouver for the victims and bringing them to Ketchikan.

I was cleared to see Rhoda the day after she got back. She was pale and had lost weight. She looked older in some ways. Her eyes no longer flashed merrily with mischief; she no longer spoke in a rush. She was sitting up in bed, chasing around a lump of Jell-O, when I walked in. At first, she didn't recognize me, then her eyes brimmed over with tears.

We had a good, long girl cry. All this time, I had been worried about her and all this time, she had thought I was dead. Reunions like this do things to you. They wipe up all the messes you made in the past, giving you a clean slate with each other. "I'm sorry I didn't listen to you," she whispered finally. "I'm sorry I wasn't braver."

I pushed back her hair and looked into her eyes. "It doesn't matter now. You're here. I'm here. We're safe. We survived."

She nodded and sniffled, rubbing at her nose. "A state trooper was in here earlier. He asked me some questions. I didn't want to answer. I don't want to talk to him, but I'll talk to you. You're still a state trooper, aren't you?"

I rolled my eyes at her, the way we did when we got caught red-handed doing something. "Maybe. They haven't decided yet. I went AWOL."

"Natalia! You're dedicated to the troopers."

"I was!" I sat close to her, no longer trying to obtain information on the most painful episode in her life but wanting to fill her in on the days we'd spent apart. "I still am, but I found I was more dedicated to you. I went into Canadian waters after you."

"You were with the Canadian Coast Guard?"

"Not quite." I winced, realizing I had already told her too much. I hedged, trying to come up with a plausible story. "How much do you remember about your last day on the yacht?" I asked testily.

She laughed and bumped up against me. "Girlfriend! There was enough of that drug inside me to rape an elephant seal!" She straightened slowly. "Wait, though. I did see something. I thought it was a hallucination, but it was on the television, so I know it's real. I saw a bear."

"Do you think it was strange the bear didn't kill you?"

"Maybe the bear thought we were dead. We were a bit comatose." She pushed aside her food tray. "What I want is a milkshake. When can you get me out of here so I can start binging?"

"I can probably get you released tomorrow. Where did you want to go, Rhoda?"

"Not back to Valdez." She frowned. "You didn't answer my question. You skirted around it. How did you track me into Canadian waters?"

I quickly retrieved the official story. "I was on an Alaskan Coast Guard vessel looking for the *Christina*, the vessel the kidnapping ring pirated."

She gave me an agonized look. "Then you saw the murdered crew?"

"You saw them, too?"

I grasped her arms and her hands went around my wrists, tightening as she spoke. "They made us look. They said it was part of our training." Her voice broke and her grip tightened.

I pressed closer to her on the bed, sharing her pain. I

loosened her grip around my wrists and held her hands in mine. "Tell me what happened after we separated."

She frowned and stared at her lap, then looked up with a cunning smile on her face. "Only if you'll tell me what you were doing on a Coast Guard vessel. That's not quite state trooper regulation."

"I told you. I was looking for you."

"Girlfriend, you had something going to pull that one off. 'Fess up."

"Okay. I'll confess. I was falling in love."

She looked surprised. "Well, about time. I wondered if you were ever going to get turned on by anybody. He must be a senior officer, for you to pull strings."

"Two of them are."

"Two of them? Now you *do* have to tell me everything."

I spent a lot of time with Rhoda over the next few days. The team had been put on shore leave, although they still had a mountain of official documenting to do that would have kept them grounded a good two weeks, anyway. This meant they spent their days between leisurely strolling around town and filling out forms on a computer.

What they weren't allowed to do, though, was spend all their time on the boat. I made sure of this. We rented a two-bedroom suite in a hotel. There was a queen-sized bed in each room that we pushed together for one super-gigantic king size. They grumbled about not being able to feel the sway of the boat, but they really liked the sleeping arrangement. We spent long hours talking about our day and how easy it would be to just settle down and live in one spot. The last part was a fantasy, but while we were recovering, it was a pleasant one.

Rhoda began to tell me her story. As she did, I relayed it to the team. The girls had been bound by their hands and shackled together with ropes when they were transported over to the coast guard vessel. They were carried like gunny sacks, dropped to the floor of the deck. They were instructed to stand and watch as the lodge was torched. A man who they were to refer to only as "drill master" told them this was part of their training. He told them they had no hope. There was nothing left behind of who they were and where they came from.

Rhoda was placed in seamen's quarters with two other girls. They each had a bunk, and there was a toilet and shower. Three times a day, the guards came and took them to the galley for a communal meal. Three hours a day, they went through training under the drill master.

The drill master was medium height, but very box-shouldered, with a thick double-chin and a scar near his left eye. "Oh, I killed him," volunteered Lee, interrupting.

"Did you really?" I asked, pausing in my story. He was laying with his head in my lap, with Darkhorse on the other side, both looking up at me as expectantly as children.

"Yeah, he looked like a nasty sort and he was crew, so..." He shrugged.

I adored everything about Lee, from his short ponytail to his playful spirit, but what I loved most was his candidness. He was as artless as a child. I rested a hand on his head as I continued. "The drill master worked on breaking them down. The girls never knew what hour of the day the drill master would come in, or which girl he would choose first for training. He only took one at a time. He would pair her with one of the other girls, but never the same one twice. When he would come for one, he would put a shock collar around her neck and lead her out with a leash."

A submerged rumble started in Josh's chest and spread to the others. "If you're going to turn into bears," I warned. "I won't finish telling you the story."

Josh grumbled but battered a pillow, then plopped it close

to my head so he could snuggle his brow next to mine. I gave him a kiss and continued.

The drill master had turned the ready room into a private theater. Two tables had been pushed together to make a stage, with the deck chairs gathered around it. Disco music played in the background.

The seat closest to the table was the captain's plush armchair, pulled from his cabin. The drill master flopped down in the deep cushions and swung a leg over one arm while the crew members filled the deck chairs. Rhoda recounted her first training session. She and another girl she had not seen before were made to get up on the table. "Dance," commanded the drill master, and Rhoda tried moving to the feverish beat. An electric shot jolted her, like the unexpected shock of touching a live circuit. "Dance better. Do man hump."

She tried again. The drill master grunted and pointed to the other girl. "You. Take off her clothes. Dancing. Man hump."

They did the bump and grind, the strange girl slowly pulling Rhoda's sweater up over her head, revealing her black-lace bra. One of the viewers cheered, "Take it off!" The girl unsnapped it from behind, letting the fabric fall to the floor. The audience demanded the girls peel away each other's clothes, item by item, while dancing provocatively to the music. When they had stripped, Rhoda was ordered, "Kiss her." Rhoda kissed the other girl hesitantly on the lips.

The drill master leaped up on the table, grabbed Rhoda by the hair with one hand, and by the tit with the other, stretching them both as far as they would go. He squeezed the nipple. "Are you hot, yet? Are you hot?" He grabbed the other girl's breasts. "Do these look hot?" He squeezed them until she cried out. "Be hot!" he warned the two menacingly. "Be hot!"

She kissed the girl again, this time, open-mouthed. "Finger her! Kiss her breasts." Swaying to the rhythm, Rhoda sucked and kissed at the girl's breasts, while her fingers slid inside the girl's crotch, massaging her moistening clit. The girl moaned and threw her head back involuntarily to the cheers of her audience.

During their days on ship, the girls were electro-shocked, their breasts pinched, and their hair pulled, but no physical marks were ever left. They were forced to give blow jobs and to dance erotically on stage, but they weren't fucked by the crew. The day before they docked at McCarthy's lodge, one of the girls rebelled. While going down on a crew member, she bit his shaft so hard, it bled. He howled, grasping his wounded dick, leapt to his feet and kicked her. When the drill master saw what she had done, he ordered all the girls out on deck and dragged the poor child to the center.

"This is what happens to willful disobedience," he announced, then wrapped his leather belt in his hand and punched her in the face. When she went down, one of the crew kicked her. Another joined in. They kept kicking her until there was nothing left but a mass of blood and tissue. They rolled her up in a blanket and threw her overboard.

There was a long silence in the room when I finished. All four of the boys were curled up so close, I couldn't tell if they were trying to comfort me or if I was supposed to be comforting them. I wasn't quite ready to get Rhoda's suffering out of my head, though. "They were made to watch Amy's rape, you know. I'm glad this will never come to trial. They never want to relive it."

Josh made a sound somewhere between a dry chuckle and a growl. "With Denisovich and the girls safe, Russia will be distancing itself from any knowledge of wrong-doing as fast as it can. We may have dumped a nightmare on Canada's lap, but we saved them from a nightmare more horrible than they can imagine."

I murmured close to his ear. "Rhoda thinks Denisovich and his men deserved what they got. She's very grateful."

"Does she know?" asked Josh, sounding a little alarmed.

I sat halfway up in bed. "Of course, she knows. She's in Ketchikan. She has a room on the next floor. Who in Ketchikan doesn't know?"

Josh put his fingers over his chest, drumming them. "It wasn't the harbor master. It wasn't the shaman. It must have been the nurse. Yep, I bet it was the nurse."

*M*ama Bear talks straight up. I don't know why it doesn't work as well for me as it does for her. I'm always being told what I should and shouldn't say. Darkhorse says it's because I have too much of a bear brain. He should talk; I'm not the one who once threw a dead log at a poacher. These things are supposed to be left up to fish and game, but there you are. Bear brain.

Josh behaved like a sacred commandment had been broken when he learned Rhoda knew we were shapeshifters. It's like Natalia said, though. The whole town knew. Some places, where they still danced and practiced the old ways, were like that. They could see straight into people, even summon their demons if they have any, and talk to the creatures inside them.

We're not a secret in some circles, and that's just the way it is. It was the government that covered us up. Once we went into services like search and rescue, firefighting and national defense, the government felt it was best to keep our shapeshifting abilities from the public. I already knew from early childhood experiences that some people really freaked out when they saw a shifter, but their concerns involved journalists, privacy, exploitation and a very long, tiring discussion on other countries and their combat readiness with shapeshifters. I think that was what bothered the government more than anything else. Shapeshifters will defend. They will rescue. But if there are shapeshifters on two sides of a war, they won't fight against each other. Animals don't go to war against other animals. So, the secret may have been to prevent shapeshifters around the world from knowing who is working for their government.

Natalia slapped me on the head for saying that, which was probably the most exciting thing a woman had ever done for me and almost made me want to give her a good roll on the spot. The government had a good point. We would not want the publicity, or the notoriety, she said. She said I couldn't imagine what it would be like if millions of people knew of our existence. That much is true. I've never been in a city larger than Anchorage, and I'm told you could drop it in the middle of San Francisco and lose it. I was a Denali villager. My tribe is Athabascan. Like the Haida, my people could peer into the shapeshifters and see their animal. They weren't millions of people, just a few thousand, and the most anyone thought about it was that bear shifters had the duty to protect and defend the tribe because they were the most powerful members. It all worked for me.

And the Coast Guard worked for me. We sailed all over the state. I've docked at so many ports, I've forgotten the names of them all. We were required for the toughest jobs; the ones battling the worst temper-tantrums Mother Nature knows how to throw, operating in areas that demanded extreme stealth and cunning. Just so you know, bears have a lot of stealth and cunning.

I didn't see any harm at all in Natalia's friend knowing we were shapeshifters. Darkhorse seemed to think it was minimal damage. "You're never going to keep local people from wagging their tongues. Some will believe the stories. Some won't. Rhoda is local."

"She remembered me, even on drugs," said Roy, puffing out his chest.

"Okay, so she knows," said Josh finally. "What should we do? Put on a performance for her?"

"No," said Natalia. "But she did give me some ideas."

We all stirred uneasily. That's what mama bears are for; to give us ideas, but ideas meant change and we liked routine. "What kind of ideas?" asked Josh, who had decided not to allow even one curly hair to grow.

"Ideas of what to do when your leave is up."

"Oh." It was a universal sigh, and we universally put our hands over our stomachs and looked at the ceiling.

Natalia folded her arms and stalked around the room. "Oh. None of you have thought past a minute beyond the next meal. In one week, your leave is up. You'll be returned to active call."

Josh tried to catch her up in his arms. "We'll be docking in Valdez. We'll still have some time together."

She pushed him away. "I'm not going back to Valdez. I'm quitting my state trooper's job."

The deflated air went through the whole room. Josh scowled. "Then what are you going to do?"

"It isn't about what I'm going to do," she said. "What are you going to do? You live on a boat. I can't just fly all over the place and meet you wherever you dock."

We're not good on the uptake when it comes to thinking things out. We usually dealt with emotional issues by popping out with furry hides, and Mama Bear didn't put up with that sort of thing. Growing a very long face and rubbing his chin, Darkhorse said, "We could build a house somewhere along the coast the way other married seamen do, someplace we can come home to."

"You mean, as if we're all married?" asked Josh, turning to face him with astonishment.

Darkhorse scratched his neck. "Basically, we are."

"Yeah." Josh began stroking Natalia's autumn wheat hair, the loosely twisting curls at the bottom wrapping around his finger. "Where would we build a house?" he asked dreamily.

"Nome," suggested Roy. "We're often in Arctic waters."

"Only in the winter," objected Josh. "And it's not the most hospitable place to live for someone like Natalia. Kodiak's a good place. I know people there. I could buy a house."

"Bristol Bay," said Natalia. "We should live in Bristol Bay. It's perfect. It has the Arctic and the Pacific spread right out in front of you. It has nice summers. And Rhoda is going out there with her new number-one boyfriend to look at the lodge he just built."

"Wait a minute," said Josh, gravel creeping into his voice. "You're not following that dizzy bitch on another adventure with another unknown man."

"He's not an unknown," she countered, shushing him with a kiss on the lips. "She's known him for three years. She only recently rotated him into the number-one position. He was the only one of her boyfriends to fly into Ketchikan to see her."

I let out my breath in a big, "Ah! So that's how they move up the line. But with us, it's all even-Steven, right?"

"Right and right," she said. "That is a good way to move up the line, and if one of you fucks up, you've all fucked up."

I'm learning. They should give girl lessons out there in the wilderness. Women are a whole different species. They talk hard, but they're soft. They act mean, but they're gentle. And they're smart. She didn't bring up the subject again that night, but she let us know what we would be missing when she was gone. I never felt a touch that caused me to tingle the way hers did. Goosebumps went up and down my spine as she kissed me on the neck and chest, her hand steadily moving downward.

I don't know how she did it, making it all about me, but giving to them as well. Her legs draped over mine like silk, yet the hands that touched her were not my own. Her fingertips traveled lightly down my arms then wrapped around my wrists as her rhythm changed from lingering strokes to the hot-throated pants of passion. She left me in a complete stupor, yet at the same time, so completely aware of how short and precious these moments of bliss truly were. She also left me feeling vulnerable, for those moments were the only times I felt completely human.

That awareness knotted up in my stomach muscles and nagged at the back of my brain like a schoolteacher. I began to regret how carelessly we had spent our early days with Natalia. We should have been storing those moments up like seashells. She wanted a house; we would build her a house. We would buy property on the moon if that was what she wanted.

When I took her in my arms, all I wanted was to satisfy her in any manner she pleased. I cupped her wonderful breasts gently, giving them the respect they deserved. I tasted the sweet honey perspiration of her flesh, buried myself deeply inside her while the red sun on her belly writhed and glowed.

She let matters rest for the night while we remained saturated with her pleasures. She didn't in the morning. Josh had a combined meeting with the harbor master and the military police, wrapping up the report on the murders, and Darkhorse was taking Roy with him to visit the district attorney concerning the kidnappings, but did not want me to come along—leaving me in the capable hands of Natalia. I figured we'd have a good jaunt through the town, maybe buy a few souvenirs, so I dressed to look sharp in my officer's uniform. It was the right call. Mama Bear gave me a smile that made me feel like a million-dollar project. She straightened my jacket at the shoulders and brushed it off. She corrected the angle of the cap and tucked back my hair. "Petty Officer Brightwater, you are to accompany me to the Pioneer Lounge."

I knew about the joint but had never been there. It was one of those places used by the sports fishermen who spent hundreds of dollars on charter boats. It was far enough from town and close enough to the sea to feel wild and adventurous, yet the first grocery store and gas station were just five minutes away. Two float planes snuggled in the small cove that curved to one side of the lounge, with two other planes perched on a small, private runway.

It was a nice enough spot. It had the standard, rustic thing going on with a central fireplace, giant windows, lots of fat leather chairs and tables set in strategically scenic spots, and a bar. The food was renowned, but it was expensive. A soda pop was expensive here, nearly three dollars for a can poured over ice.

Despite its name, the Pioneer didn't cater to locals. It catered to tourists. Practically everybody in the lounge looked up and turned their heads when they saw an officer of the Coast Guard walk in with a local girl by his side. Some even whispered to each other. Teenagers in short shorts and puffy vests, dying of boredom in the wild setting, twisted the ends of their hair and twittered between themselves when they saw me. The out-of-shape wives of the sportsmen, positive they wanted the Great Alaskan Adventure until they experienced it, looked at Natalia with their lips compressed angrily together as though she was personally responsible for luring their men into untamed country.

I thought we were going to have one of those cappuccinos she likes so much, then leave, but instead of walking toward a table, she waited by the bar until someone with a familiar scent came up behind us and tinkled, "Natalia, you made it—and you managed to drag one of your boys along. He's gorgeous. Are you going to introduce us?"

I swiveled my stool away from the bar to face her. Rhoda looked a lot better than when she was first brought home. She had looked like a rubber doll, her face waxy, her eyes dull and vague. Now, she was clean and healthy again. She had the kind of prettiness you see in prom queens—nice skin, girlish features, dimples, big smile full of perfect ivory teeth. She was a little smaller than Natalia and she fiddled more with her hair and make-up. I guess she was a more stylish dresser, too, but Natalia still outshone her—in my opinion, at least.

"Rhoda, meet Lee. He did visit you in the hospital, but you probably don't remember."

"I don't want to remember," said Rhoda. "I've remembered all I need to for as long as I've needed and now, I'm going to forget everything I can."

I had to admire the girl. She was resilient. She was also Natalia's best friend, so I needed to put on some manners. "Should I order drinks?" I asked.

Her voice tinkled again, this time in light laughter. "No, it's too early for that. We've got a table over by the far window." She pulled at my arm. "Come on. I want you to meet Drew Petty."

Now I got it. I was being ambushed by this nefarious new invader into Natalia's life. He would try to get me on his side, thinking all was well, but I would show him I was no push-over. My resolve isn't the greatest in the world. As soon as I saw him, I liked him. He didn't look all that pretentious, just successful—a successful millennial. A tie slid down an expensive silk shirt, the knot two inches below the open collar. His sleeves were rolled up, revealing a tattoo that began at the wrist and traveled up under his shirt, ending at the neck. He had one of those crisp, shiny haircuts you get in salons, and crisp black eyes measuring me from light-reflective glasses. The fancy ones that turned lighter or darker as needed.

He liked talking about himself. He was originally from Seattle and had made his way through college working fishing boats. He'd received his small airplane pilot's license shortly after graduation and made his first million four years later with a game that gave a real-life simulation of flying into the wilderness.

"Now I own my own plane," he told me. "I've been flying for these guys for a while, but I like the Bristol Bay area better. It has its own energy. All these islands. They're a bit like a jungle. The majestic skies, that's what I'm aiming for."

"And bears," giggled Rhoda. "Drew wants to be where there are more bears."

Just then, Natalia received a phone call. She texted in a message and said, "The captain and the others are on their way over."

"Oh, the guests here will be talking about us for the rest of the day," whispered Rhoda, leaning across the table. "Imagine, four Coast Guard officers here in full uniform."

"They know what we are?" I whispered back in controlled alarm.

Rhoda rested her chins on her fists and grinned. "They

know you're seamen. How often do you think real seamen come in here?"

I heaved a sigh of relief and sat back, straightening my uniform even more. That was acceptable. I returned to my conversation with Drew. "What's wrong with Ketchikan bears?"

Drew chuckled and ordered two double-shot espressos. Now, that's what I'm talking about. None of this stuff shot through with air and milk. Real coffee, more concentrated than the cook's poisonous brew. "There's nothing wrong with Ketchikan's bears," he said. "But the tourists want to see big bears. Northern bears."

"Like me," I said without thinking.

"Like Katmai bears," Natalia said hastily.

"Of course," said Drew, smiling but giving me a knowing look. "Like Katmai bears."

My anxieties were beginning to drive me through the roof. There were all these rules about what I was and wasn't supposed to say among non-Native people and what I couldn't say to non-local people. It was too complicated, and I was flopping around like a flounder in the bottom of a boat. I let out an audible sigh of relief when the captain and the rest of the team appeared.

"So," Drew continued, as soon as introductions had been made and everyone was seated comfortably. "I bought a piece of property about sixty miles from Dillingham. It already has a small lodge on it, but it needs improvement. I'm going to make it bigger. It's going to have a lounge, guest rooms, fishing guide and charter boat services, bear viewing tours. Natalia is looking for a job, so I'm hiring her."

"Why Natalia?" asked Josh suspiciously. He was still rankling over the kidnapping ring and wasn't much into trusting anybody. He automatically put a protective arm around her. Always one to think about our unity, I pressed close to Natalia, too, and gave Drew my best scowl.

"She's a people person," explained Drew. "And she thinks on her feet. She's a survivalist. Rhoda told me all about her, and of how she rescued that girl, Amy. That's the type of person I want running my lodge."

"And Natalia agreed to this?" There was an audible rumble in the captain's throat.

"On one condition." Drew pushed away his cup and gave all of us a straight-up look. "You have to invest with me. She said you were looking for a location to build your house—here's your location. I need a business partner to make this work. I don't have the funds to cover the entire lodge, plus staff and expenses. It's a business venture, maybe a gamble."

Darkhorse pulled at his chin, making one of those very long faces he made when he was thinking. "Not a big business venture for us. We all have our Coast Guard income. We were going to build her a house, anyway."

"A house on the coastline, so we have a place to go to when we're off-duty," agreed the captain. "Would the costs be much more?"

"The upkeep, maybe," hedged Drew. "Unless we can draw a good clientele. We need people to talk about us. Word-of-mouth is the best advertisement."

The captain's brow was growing dangerously thick. "We don't do anything illegal."

Drew made a placating gesture. "I know you don't. I admire and uphold the law. Would I hire someone like Natalia if I didn't?"

"Oh, she would so kick your ass if you didn't," I muttered.

He gave a nervous laugh and wiped at his neck. "Here's the thing." He waved us all in closer, so we were leaning over the table like conspiring politicians. "People want to see bears. They want to see them up close and photograph them, but they don't want to see them in a zoo. They want to see them in the wild. And wild bears are dangerous."

This was a fact we could agree upon. Katmai bears had gotten used to being photographed, but they could still be unpredictable, and the reserve was a two-hour flight from the lodge location. There were a lot of Bristol Bay bears, but historically, they weren't very nice. Most lodges discouraged them from coming too close to prevent possible mayhem and murder.

"I was thinking," he said, dropping his voice even lower, "that since you will be there on shore leave, you could stalk around the property in bear form."

"Bear form?" asked Darkhorse innocently.

"Yeah," put in Rhoda. "Prowl around the perimeter. Keep the grounds safe and, at the same time, give our guests a good look at bears."

Josh made a dangerous sound in his throat, and Natalia quickly put her hands over his. "They know, Captain. They both know. Let it go."

"They would never know you were shifters," pointed out Drew. "Maybe you could even do a few neat bear tricks."

This time the rumble was very menacing. "Okay, no tricks," he retracted nervously. "But there are documented cases of bears opening and drinking beer. Would you mind if I left out a cooler?"

"Bears drinking beer is natural," said Darkhorse. That sounded about right, so I nodded my head up and down vigorously.

"A cooler is acceptable," agreed Josh. He was starting to get into it. We could be adaptable when the necessity arose, and this seemed like a necessity. If we had to do a little bear flashing to keep Natalia happy, it wasn't such a bad idea. "Perimeter watching. Occasional kitchen invasions. No mass media advertising, however. No attaching the name of the lodge to any viral clips. No cute tricks."

Now I know why there are businesspeople and lawyers. Ordinary people couldn't possibly imagine all the things that might come up in a partnership or a venture. We spent the next three days working out a verbal agreement that was formally drafted out after we had a chance to look at the property. The one structure on the property was a two-story cabin with a sharply pitched roof. It was solid and wouldn't take much to add onto it. The ground was also clear and ready for development.

I believed Captain Josh pulled some strings. We got stationed in Homer that winter, making it easy to fly out to the lodge and check on its progress when we weren't busy pulling boats out of the ice or catching drug runners. Three months after our first visit, crammed into a Homer café with two lawyers, a banker, and an accountant, we signed the official documents that made us part owners to a Bristol Bay lodge. There was an enormous amount of "whoever" and "do agree" that I was expected to initial at the end of reading each paragraph, implying I understood something that was as impossible to imagine as millions of people.

We finally muddled through. Mama Bear had put her foot down and said she wanted a home, and we made her a home just where she wanted it. Every chance we got, we flew in or sailed into the sweet harbor of her embrace. We enjoyed entertaining the guests in our bear form. Sometimes, we ripped off the best pastries in the kitchen, drank beer out on the lawn or made faces in the windows at the kids, but no tricks. We weren't anybody's tame bears, coming at beck and call.

It's odd how my life has been. First, I had a simple life; then a double life. Then, my life became so complicated, I didn't know my head from my feet. Natalia made it all harmonious. I realized I didn't have to struggle to become part of something; I already was a member of the clan. I didn't have to understand all the wherefore and whoever—I only had to understand my heart.

We had a lot of adventures ahead of us. That year, we had to chase down a shapeshifting wolverine that had run amok in the northern villages… but that's another story. This one is about Natalia, and how she became the mama bear that kept us glued together.

I didn't like to think about the future because I knew that the day we parted with Natalia, my heart would ache so much, the tears would fall. Natalia forced me to look at it and make plans for it, and I was glad that she did. I didn't ordinarily like businesspeople, but Drew wasn't a true corporate millionaire. He hung on the edge, his self-enterprise a crash or boom. Of course, with Natalia drawn in, I wanted him to boom.

It was difficult at first. All we had was a remote cabin under construction, our ship, and short periods of time with Natalia. She found an apartment, and for that first winter, we had to adjust to solid ground under our feet when we weren't sailing. Only the sound of the ocean and the comfort of her arms helped me sleep when I was on shore.

Nothing was more difficult than the first time we set sail, leaving Natalia at the Homer harbor, promising to be there when we returned. My heart left me and stayed right there on that Homer spit until I returned. When my heart and I were reunited, my tears did fall. They rained all over her. I promised her I would do everything she asked. I signed all the paperwork and that spring, we were building a house for Mama Bear.

Drew was right about Natalia as the overseer for the lodge. She was personable—not as bubbling as Rhoda, who was the hostess, but personable in the way of a professional instructor. She made a good trail guide. She taught survival skills. She knew how to handle an emergency. There was "state trooper" written all over her attitude, so people behaved.

She met us at the dock in Homer every time our boat came in while the lodge was in its first stages, but by the second year, it was no longer necessary. The building was finished. We moved out of the apartment. We had summer-long clientele, with flights and charters. In the winter, we used one of our company's cubs to fly across the bay to our home.

Our home. We built our house separate from the lodge and in line with a small group of cabins. It had looked like a small community in the summer, although in the winter, it was nearly deserted. Only a few of the staff members with no place to go, some international travelers wanting some northern exposure, and an occasional local checking out the scene hung out at the lodge during the winter. If Natalia minded the solitude, she didn't say anything about it. She was never completely alone. Even if she saw the same faces day after day, there were villages nearby. She would some-times take out one of the boats to go visiting. On calm days, she would fly into Homer with the cook for supplies and a short holiday.

You wouldn't think that small amount of visiting with other Bristol Bay residents would have changed things, but it did. Since Natalia had gone to visit them, some of the villagers decided to visit her. On at least one occasion, some villagers came out while my team and I were romping around as bears.

When the Natives start seeing shapeshifters, word gets out. By the end of the second year, locals from miles around were visiting the lodge and holding their dances. They began having shapeshifters reunions. The pull of their chants, the rhythm of their drums was too much for us. The tourists enjoyed seeing them in the summer, but in the winter, the sound of the drums and the steady chants became too much for us. We became a part of it. We joined the dance by the flickering firelight while our bear shadows stood straight and tall. The wolves howled and the eagles soared. The raven watched until dawn.

There is a story—perhaps you've heard it—that a shapeshifter can tell a mama bear by a little piece of red sun glowing in her stomach, given to her by a raven. The first time I made love to Natalia, I saw that red glow. I knew we were destined for her. Oh, hell. I knew it the minute I was a raging shapeshifting bear standing in front of her for the first time, scaring the piss out of her. I could feel the pull of that red sun. Darkhorse knew. He'd also felt that irresistible pull and was ready to sacrifice himself to her right there on the spot. It's why he let her beat him into submissiveness. They all knew. Natalia was a mama bear and we could never be anything else except the loyal shapeshifters who loved her.

The night of the winter solstice, the shapeshifters gathered from hundreds of miles around to celebrate the returning sun. It was a night when all spirit animals can be released, even the ones so deeply hidden, the hosts never realize they are there. I felt so wild and free, among a people who understood me. I danced feverishly, my heart pounding, my skin shining with sweat in the firelight.

I was mesmerized by Natalia. She was in a strange, moving trance. Her eyes smoldered, her slightly parted lips glistened, her skin was glossy in the flow of the flames. Surrounding her were the other bear forms, their shadows leaping as high as the trees. They wove in and out, keeping a steady beat, seeming to touch her but backing away. Another pass around the fire and they came closer, sniffing the air while she danced, her hips twisting, her breath rushing in and out excitedly.

The chanters squatted low to the ground, hands fluttering in front of them, working their magic. I was hypnotized. I felt a passion like none I had experienced before. I could think of nothing except my burning desire to drown in her embraces, to sink into her arms forever. I gathered her up and carried her away with the rest of the team still circling around her, giving of themselves without taking, waiting for the moment that belonged to all of us. I carried her to our cabin while the wolves howled, the ravens cackled, and the other shapeshifters continued their unworldly dance between animal and human.

The sky remained still and black. The promise of a returning red sun was a dim memory in a night twenty-one hours long. The shifting northern lights cast down long spears of color that dazzled the pale, distant moon. She looked ethereal under a sky so brilliant with colors, it turned the landscape blue. I set her inside our newly finished home. She was wearing a long, embroidered parka that she unzipped and let drop to the floor. We surrounded her and touched her soft under garments. They slipped away under our hands, revealing creamy flesh that curved in gracefully at the neck and waist and spread with buttery smoothness to full, upright breasts and flaring hips.

We carried her to the bed especially made for the five of us and set her down tenderly, accepting her caressing touch and approaching only when she drew us closer. We began to merge. Our touches. Our thoughts. Our saliva mixed in a tangle of arms and legs, in a swell of emotions that heaved with both turbulence and ecstasy. We were each other and we were one.

Outside the windows, the drums were still beating, still calling back the red sun. The sounds echoed into the forest and were picked up again as village after village answered. I kissed the red spot on Natalia's flat stomach. It was just under and to the right of her heart, and it was glowing.

Three months went by and the glow spread. She became irritable. She threw up in the morning and ate everything in sight for the rest of the day. She was demanding. She would complain that she was cold and when we turned into bear rugs to keep her warm, complained that she was hot.

Three of the village elders came to see her. One of them, an old lady who used a walker to get around and painted her nails with glittering purple polish, felt Natalia's forehead, patted her tummy, and shrugged. "That's easy enough. She's pregnant."

That was easy enough for a diagnosis, but it still presented a problem. The elders huddled together and held a consultation. The old lady, who must have been their own mama bear, spoke again. "You can't take her to Homer. You can't take her to a regular doctor."

"No, I don't suppose we can," I agreed, scratching the back of my neck and trying to decide whether I should look happy or worried.

It wasn't the right response. Natalia shouted unhappily, "Well, I'm not going to have the baby by myself."

The old lady cranked over her walker to stand by Natalia reassuringly. "We'll send a specialist. She has experience with shapeshifter babies."

Natalia wasn't the cheeriest of patients. "I hope you don't expect me to live in a cave for six months," she responded sulkily, then winced. "Although hibernating wouldn't be bad. Aren't bear cubs supposed to be tiny?"

The old lady chuckled, her walker scraping against the floor as she moved around. "It's your body adjusting. Relax. Don't worry. We've got you covered."

The elders had said not to worry, so I put on a hopeful, happy face after they left. "You're not sick! You're going to have a baby. That's good news."

She glanced at the four of us, all with the same ear-to-ear grin. "I knew I was pregnant. I was just afraid to say some-thing," she confided sulkily.

I scowled, puzzled. "Why?"

"You're on duty. You might not be here when the baby is born. I've been trying to work it out. Do shapeshifters even look human when they're born? A lot of things run through my head."

I sat next to her and held her hand. "You won't be alone. The village is sending their expert."

She gave me a dubious look. "A medicine woman?"

"A midwife who delivers shapeshifter babies. And I'll put in a special request with the admiralty to rotate our leave so one of us is always home."

She looked hopeful instead of irritable for the first time in three months. "You can do that?"

"I will do that. Can you allow us to be happy now? We're going to have a baby!"

"Yes," she said, "you can be happy."

She followed us to the front door and stood on the porch to watch as we tumbled into the yard. It was a glorious, early spring day. No clientele had come in yet and only the staff were at the lodge, preparing it for the first customers. We popped into bear form and did somersaults and jumps that tore holes in the walkway that had been freshly filled with gravel. We accidentally uprooted a young lilac tree. We lifted the corner of a cabin without realizing there was a staff member inside, cleaning it out. When we settled it back on its pilings, the worker flew out screaming words I wouldn't expose a street rat to, chucking a few rocks our way before stalking into the lodge and slamming the door. I looked toward Natalia. She was laughing so hard, tears rolled down her eyes.

She didn't pop out during the summer months and was her usual busy self for the tourist season, taking clientele on their adventure of a lifetime without even one of them realizing she was an expectant mother. We weren't off-duty as much as we would have liked, but there was nearly always one of us to stay with her and keep her safe. She was happier that way and began to hum a lot while she puttered around the house.

As it turned out, we all got to be there for the big event. The winter storms were late in moving in, so the cutter stood idle at the pier, without even a tourist in distress to warrant firing its engines. We were enjoying our time at home. Every day we spent there became more a part of us than all the years we had spent on the ocean.

After she stopped having morning sickness, Natalia did feel better. She made us rearrange the entire house, beginning with clearing out the junk we'd accumulated in the spare room and turning it into a baby room. We also had to pick up all our electronic equipment and confine it to the office. She didn't care if we were battling online ogres or charting a course through the Northwest Passage, it belonged in one room. There was also baby-proofing, which wasn't going to do much good if the baby was a shapeshifter, but I didn't tell her. She had enough on her mind.

She was different at night, though. She was reluctant to let us see her body. She thought it was ugly. As her stomach swelled, the red spot grew larger and glowed more deeply.

The spot pulsed, wonderfully round and brimming with life. It was beautiful. It always took a long time to convince her of that, a long time to coax her into letting us pull back her clothing and view her beautiful swelling, to rub it and feel the child growing. It was magical and precious. At last, we convinced her how much we loved even her swelling belly, because it was part of what made our mama bear so complete.

We really thought we had it together. We had cleaned, baby-proofed, practiced all kinds of relaxation exercises and control routines, and, as I said, were miraculously all available when the big day came. For all our preparation, the day she went into labor, we were gripping the walls to keep from falling apart. After what seemed like three days and nights but was somehow only twelve hours, the midwife delivered a tiny baby girl.

"Four pounds, I'd say," she told me as she wrapped up the itty-bitty thing and placed it in my arms. "Let's see how the other one comes out." She knelt back down on the floor between Natalia's legs.

I felt the blood rush from my head like I was going to faint. It had been hard enough watching Natalia go through twelve hours of mortal agony, and now the midwife was saying there was something else! "The other one?" I stammered.

She sniffed. "You bear. Don't you know anything about your mamas? They're always putting out twins."

"Maybe the other one will be a boy," Lee said hopefully. "I have a twin sister. She doesn't look like me, though, and she's not a shapeshifter."

"Happens. Happens." The midwife waited until Natalia threw out an extra-long curse then pushed so hard, her fingernails bit into my hand as she squeezed it. "Hah," she said with apparent satisfaction. "Identical twins."

"I have twin girls?" asked Natalia, a trembling smile on her lips. "They are girls?" She laid back with a sigh of relief and half-closed her eyes dreamily. "Then they won't be shapeshifters."

The midwife scoffed. "Who says they won't be shapeshifters?"

Cleaned and swaddled, the babies had been given to Natalia. They snuggled together in her arms, their little heads nuzzling against her breasts. They had soft, angel hair, golden on top but turning to brown. She stroked a golden-topped head. "Aren't the shapeshifters all men?"

"My mother was a shapeshifter," said Roy, popping her bubble.

"There are a lot of shapeshifting women in my family," added Darkhorse. "Sometimes, it seemed there were more shapeshifting women than there were men, but not here. There are never enough women around here, shapeshifter or human."

"Are you bears?" Natalia whispered to the twins, but they just nuzzled her like babies.

We named them Kelly and Layla. Somehow, Natalia thought giving them perky, modern girls names would prevent them from turning into shapeshifters. At first, it seemed like she worried for nothing. They looked like ordinary human babies, until they began crawling. Then, instead of crawling on their knees, they semi-shifted so that they had haunches and stiff back legs. Natalia saw it but pretended she didn't, preferring to look away and tell herself the girls were normal.

It wasn't until their first birthday that they fully shifted, however. The cook had baked a gigantic cake and invited the entire staff to the party. Everything was fine until the enormous treat was placed in front of the twins. With the first whiff, the girls turned into bears and gobbled down the cake.

Mama Bear has her work cut out. It's a good thing there is always someone there with her. Lately, the twins have been escaping to play in the yard as bears. Fortunately, the tourists haven't seen them shift. They just think it's exciting to see bear cubs on swing sets and going down slides, and never once question where the mama bear might be.

Natalia's a little unhappy right now. We're being called away on another mission and we'll have to leave our mama bear and beautiful girls for a while. But she won't be alone. Rhoda and Drew will be there. They got married last year, so I guess Rhoda officially cut off her line of waiting men.

Still, my heart breaks every time I'm away from her. Take it from a seaman; there is nothing better than a woman who takes you in her arms when you arrive home from the sea. It's an enormous ocean, one murmuring with secrets and lashing with rage. It has a will of its own.

We're bound for the Chukchi Sea in the deep northern regions, where the sea lions play and walrus bask in the setting sun. A group of scientists had been exploring Lawrence Island and said they found the remains of an ancient civilization. They were given a grant to document the findings. They claimed to have found the first evidence of a mermaid city, but they haven't been heard from in three weeks. They are probably lost.

Standing at the captain's helm, I ordered the engineer to fire up the engines. The cutter chugged out into the wide Bristol Bay. I chuckled. Mermaids! Wouldn't you know it? It takes all kinds.

Thank you for reading Natalia's story! For another steamy reverse harem tale, pick up the next book in the series now!

Mated to the Clan

books2read.com/matedtotheclan

Ellie thought getting away to a remote mountain town would bring her some much needed peace and quiet except now she's fending off advances from four gorgeous mountain men…

Keep reading for a sneak peek of the next book!

MATED TO THE CLAN

The air brakes of the bus hissed as the vehicle jolted. My head hit the seat before me, waking me from my travel-fevered sleep.

"Ouch."

"Watch it, lady," groused the passenger ahead of me.

"Oh, for heaven's sake," I muttered. It wasn't my fault the vehicle stopped suddenly.

"What did you say?" said the man. He twisted and squinted at me angrily.

"I said I pray to the good Lord I don't have occasion to use the hunting knife in my backpack." I gave him a sunshiny smile to put on a psycho air, but I also know bus drivers don't play when it comes to disagreements. We could both get booted off. Mr. Angry Man seemed aware of this too, and with a glance to the driver, he grunted and put his eyes forward.

Reflexively, I fingered my mother's locket, something she always wore, and now I wore in memory of her. Her passing two months ago hit me hard. I missed her horribly and the fact that I was running from my past once again did nothing for my mood.

Buses are a long, hard way to get somewhere, but if you travel to the middle of nowhere and have no car of your own, they're a necessary evil. On either side on this two-lane highway is a wall of green that claimed the broken back of the Appalachian Mountains. The right side was mostly one long stretch of tree line that climbed the slopes of a mountain range eaten away by a half billion years of existence. Along the left, the land tumbled steeply into a one of the uncounted long lakes of the region. The only relief was the occasional house, or a reddish-brown farm stand clinging to the side of the highway, as if cutting into the interior represented some great danger. Every minute of the ride stretched out as if the Universe expected you to examine the beginning and end in infinite detail before you could pick up the next moment of time.

That's why my lids grew heavy, and I leaned my head between the crack of the seat and wall of the bus, cushioned by my jacket.

"Hurry, Ainsley, hurry."

"Wha—" I'm half-asleep and my mother is trying to lift me, but I'm a big girl. Daddy said so. "What's wrong, Mommy?"

"We've got to go now."

"Mrs. Lane, we have to hurry."

I stared in the eyes of the big man who stood next to Mommy. His clothes were dark, and he sort of looked like a policeman. The policeman came to school often, and he was nice. This man—I don't like him. Mommy looked scared.

A motorbike rumbled on the street. Daddy's coming home.

"Oh God," Mommy gasped.

"I'll get her. You get to the van."

The big man picked me up, and I kicked and screamed. Daddy was coming home, and I wanted to see him. I was so upset and crying because the man was taking me away from my daddy that I forgot Ginger Bear.

"Ginger Bear! Ginger Bear! I want my bear!" I screamed as the man put me in the black van and climbed in as Mommy snapped on my seatbelt.

"We'll get you another one," she said.

"Go!" called the man. The van lurched forward, and I screamed in my fright.

My head hit the back of the forward seat again but it seemed now I reached my destination.

"Clarkstown!" called the driver.

I gathered my backpack and my jacket, checking twice before I walked away. Since that night, I always checked twice before I left a place. If I lost something, I might not get the chance to retrieve it again.

Much of my life was like that. We moved to more places than I could remember. I didn't understand until I was older that the person we ran from was my father. I didn't know what a bad man he was.

Dangerous.

Criminal.

Wanted.

Road weariness sizzled through my bones as I stepped shakily from the bus. The driver had pulled my luggage, and it sat forlorn on the ground.

"Is that it?" he said.

"Yes."

He looked at me expectantly, and I dug into my pocket for a dollar, the last one I had. There was some money in my online account. But things looked grim in the one-street town, tenanted with one large building whose sign marked it as the General Store, and a single gas station. I may not find an ATM to draw out some cash here.

Maybe it was better that way.

He glanced at the dollar and twisted his mouth in disapproval but screw him. I wasn't flush with cash, and I would not spend it like I was.

"Thanks for a pleasant ride," I said as I picked up the luggage. He grumbled and climbed the stairs to his seat. There wasn't even a rest stop for him and the other passengers before he rolled out leaving me behind.

With a groan of tires on gravel, the bus pulled away, and a man stood at the doorway of the gas station. It wasn't hard to notice him. Apparently, they grow them big here in Maine because this guy was six-one of solid muscle with a jaw square enough to cut glass. His green eyes twinkled from under a baseball cap.

"You must be Ellie."

"I am."

He walked forward and stuck out his hand. I offered mine, and he took it, covering my tiny hand completely, but instead of squeezing it, sheltered it with its warmth. I looked up into his eyes and saw only welcome.

"Cole Clark."

"Nice to meet you, Mr. Clark."

"Cole."

"Ellie Harper."

He smiled slowly and broadly as if he hid a secret. "I thought we established that already."

My eyes narrowed. This guy wasn't poking fun at me, was he? And no, I am not nervous. There's no reason to be even if the most gorgeous guy I've ever seen is holding my hand. Those butterflies fluttering in my stomach are from too much coffee and too little food in the past three days.

"I'll take that," he said, releasing my hand and reaching for my luggage exactly at the same time as my stomach squelched in its underfed state.

"Our next stop is the General Store. You best stock up on

whatever eats you want because I only come into town once a week."

"Um, ah," I said, my face turning red because it suddenly washed over me how ignorant I was about my present surroundings. "Does it take debit cards?"

He smiled amused by my naivete.

"Debit cards?" he asked as if he never heard of them.

Oh shit. What the hell would I do now?

The door of the gas station opened, and a man bigger than Cole in a sheriff's uniform stepped out holding a cup of coffee and walked to us. He was six-two at least, with arms that look liked they'd seen plenty of time in the gym or hauling logs. One never knew in the middle of nowhere in Maine.

"This man bothering you, ma'am?" he said with an air of authority that did not brook disrespect.

"Sheriff," said Cole coolly. "Ms. Harper just asked if the General Store took debit cards."

"And you asked what debit cards are," he said with a rumble of disapproval.

Cole gave a slight shrug of his shoulders.

"So, you *are* bothering her. No wonder the census is down at the lodge if you keep harassing the customers. And you the manager. Apologize to Ms. Harper."

Wow. Law-and-order in Clarkstown extended to enforcing courtesy. This sheriff was a hard-ass.

Instead Cole chuckled.

"Ms. Harper, meet Sheriff Zain Clark, my cousin and co-owner of the Clarkstown Lodge."

"Damn straight," rumbled Zain.

"Nice to meet you, Sheriff."

"Call me, Zain. We *will* share digs."

Sharing? What?

The Sheriff's eyes glinted with mischief, and I got that for the second time in two seconds I got played.

"Who's pulling her leg now?" said Cole with exasperation in his voice. "You have your own cabin, Ms. Harper. In fact, I've started up the wood stove already so it will be nice and cozy when we get there. No, Zain, and my other two cousins, Marcus and Drew, live at the main lodge with me. But since guests usually spend most of their time in the lodge, it's easy to think we are living together. But don't worry, Zain has promised not to harass the guests this season."

"Says who?" said Mr. Law-and-Order with a smile.

"Let's go, Ellie, before he cuffs us for his own amusement."

"He does that?"

"He wishes," snorted Cole.

"I'll see you later," said Zain smiling. "Oh, and to answer your question, Ms. Harper, the cashless society follows us even into the depth of Maine's woods. Your debit card works at any of Clarktown's fine establishments."

"Yeah," said Cole. "All three."

ZAIN

$\mathcal{I}$t was a busy day, so there was no time to think about the adorable woman that rented a cabin from us. I forgot what Cole said about how long she'd stay. Cole told me she wanted a quiet place to work. Most of our female guests were twenty years older. Now I wish I had listened more because I could see how five foot-seven of blond hair and curves could spice things up.

I purposely ignored that this was precisely what I berated Cole for regularly. He fell in love at least once a summer and built a sizable little black book for hook-ups. Somehow the women never stuck to Cole, they knew he wasn't long-term material. But they would need to leave city life behind and move in with a backwoodsman and his three cousins. So, Cole remained the "summer attraction" for the lodge, a role that we all disparaged and secretly envied.

Well, everyone but me.

No.

Really.

I pulled the cruiser over to the General Store which doubled as the government center of our little town. The post office was there, as well as a single room we shared with the town clerk, Mrs. Ahern, who only kept office hours three days a week. Drew was there, going through the mail.

"Hey," he said brightening when he spotted me. "Have you heard about the bear and the stripper?"

"Probably," I said as I lifted the hinged part of the counter that let me into the desk area. "You've regaled me with every one of your jokes at least five times.

"Then, why did the turtle cross the road?"

I picked up the mail and flipped through it. "Ask Marcus. He's the game warden of the family."

"You're no fun," he complained, and I arched an eyebrow at his remark.

"Okay, here's a new one. A little law enforcement humor."

I sat at my desk and pressed the power button on my computer. "Go ahead," I said, hoping he kept this short. If Drew got the jokes out his system now, my cousin would slow down for the rest of the day.

"Get this. A man breaks into a home in the middle of the night and searches for valuables with a flashlight when he hears a voice say, 'Jesus is watching you.' Startled, the man looks around quickly, but doesn't see anything, so he continues his search. He goes to pick up a stereo when he hears again, 'Jesus is watching you.'

"Now freaking out, the thief scans the room more carefully for the source of the warning and sees a parrot on a perch in the corner. The thief then whispers, 'Was that you?'

"The parrot replies, 'Yes, it was.'

"Amused with the bird, the thief says, 'Thanks for the warning, but I'm an atheist. So, what's your name?' And the parrot answers, 'Moses.'

"Now laughing out loud, the thief asks, 'What kind of people name a parrot Moses?' And the parrot replies, 'The same kind that name their Rottweiler Jesus.'"

"Uh huh," I said.

"What? Not even a little funny?"

"No. Hey, did you pull the recent most-wanted off the FBI site?" I stared at one face, a one percenter biker on the run for drug trafficking, and he seemed familiar. I glanced at the name—Xavier Lane. Nope. Don't know him,, but I sent it to the laser printer so I can stick it on the bulletin board.

"Like one of them will show up here."

"I don't know. It's easy to get lost on the Trail. Marcus told me last night that some hikers complained to him about some suspicious characters hanging out on the Trail."

"Uh, huh," Drew said, unconvinced. "One. It's too damn cold at night right now to sleep up there. Two. Hikers aren't likely to come across hardcore mountain men waiting for someone to find them suspicious."

"That is exactly what I told Marcus. But you can't be too careful."

"Did you see the request from Dunlop County for extra help during their Motorbike Festival?"

I had pushed the request aside. We are a two-man operation for four thousand, though mostly uninhabited, square miles. I didn't like sending one of us off to another county.

"Yes."

"I'd like to go."

"No."

"Things have been quiet here, and to tell you the truth, I'm a little bored."

"In that case—no."

"Alpha asshole," Drew grumbled, turning back to his computer.

The office door swung open, and Marcus entered.

"Hi, Stumpy," Drew greeted, in rare form today. "Did you hear the one—"

Marcus drew the unfortunate nickname of Stumpy since

he went to the SUNY School of Forestry. The denizens of that school tended to suffer that nickname.

"Yes."

"But you didn't even—"

"Yeah, I did. You talk in your sleep. Loudly. Right through the walls."

"I do not," Drew said .

"Suit yourself. But I now know your passwords for your phone and your laptop."

"You do not."

Marcus chuckled. "But now, just to be sure, you'll have to change them anyway."

"Bastard," Drew muttered as he pulled his phone out.

"And this," said Cole loudly, "is the Sheriff's and Town Clerk's office." The office door swung open once more, and I swear every pair of eyes fell on Ellie Harper.

Ellie stared at us as if she'd never seen four men in the same room together.

"Well," said Marcus, "who is this?"

"This is our newest guest, Ellie Harper," said Cole, narrowing his eyes at Marcus. "Ellie, this is our local game warden, Marcus Clark."

"Another Clark man in uniform," she mused.

"At your service."

"I suppose you're another cousin as well?"

"Guilty. Now I see why smoke rose from the chimney of the Moose cottage this morning."

"Moose cottage?" said Ellie. "There's not a moose head hanging on the wall, is there? I couldn't stay in a cottage with a dead thing staring at me."

"Sure there is," said Drew brightly. Cole gave him a cutting glance that would have shut up any smart person.

"We'll make sure," I said, "that we take it down for the duration. It's our nicest cottage, and we wouldn't want you to miss that. Marcus, on your way out to patrol, can you stop by and take the moose head down?"

"Sure, Zain, no problem." He gave Cole a smug smile that said 'Hey, I'm scoring points with the lady.' Cole, standing behind Ellie, bared his teeth.

"Thank you, Marcus," I said. "That would be helpful. Cole, do you need help with the supplies?"

"No. I'm good."

"I'll give you a hand anyway. Drew, print out the new most-wanteds and post them. I'm going to check out Marcus' concern on the trail."

"I'll go with," said Drew. "I've sat in the office too long."

"No. I'm fine. Someone has to man the office while Mrs. Ahern is out. And tell the Sheriff of Dunlop County that you'll go help them out."

"Wait? What's the catch?"

"No catch. We're just showing solidarity for our brothers in law enforcement." I pulled my trooper hat off the hat rack. "Call me if anything happens."

"Yeah," said Marcus. "Let us know about your new high score on Warcraft."

"You wish you could do as well at Warcraft."

"Bye, Drew," I said.

"So," Ellie said as we walked the hallway to the front of the store. "All of you are cousins? And you live together?"

"The lodge," said Cole, "is part of the family trust. Clarks have lived on the land for one hundred and twenty-five years."

"That's impressive. I haven't lived anywhere—well, never mind. The pictures on your website are gorgeous. I can't wait to see it."

"I look forward to showing you around," said Cole.

Damn, Mr. Charm had zeroed in on her already. For reasons beyond my understanding, this time I mind. This is not like me at all. And then, me sending Drew off to the motorcycle rally? Why the hell would I do that?

"Cole, how are the repairs going on the cabins?"

"Fine. We have weeks before Memorial Day."

"Is that when your usual season starts?" asks Ellie.

"Our summer season. We have the hunting season and ski season and keep busy in various parts of the year. The middle of January and February is when we get snowed in, and the cabins need a little TLC after they've been vacant during the winter."

"Yeah," chuckled Marcus. "We have to de-critter them."

"De-critter?"

"Deep woods version of decluttering," said Cole. "Don't worry. Your cabin is cleaned and ready."

We all hauled boxes of groceries to the truck. I couldn't help but watch Ellie - her smile, how her body moved, and the bear inside me rumbled his approval. This was not the right time for my animal self to rouse from his winter hibernation and take notice. I'm the Alpha, the leader of the clan, but I was always calmest during winter hibernation when my beast slept and waited for spring. But Ellie roused him in a way other women hadn't.

I was in big trouble.

Epic World Building Academy Romance

The Broken Academy

Power of Fire

Power of Magic

Power of Blood

Pacts & Promises

Bonds

Reverse Harem Escapes – Great for a Quick Roll in the Hay with None of the Guilt

The Descendants :

Shared by the Four

Desired by Four

Fate of Three

Fated Shifter Mates

Mated to the Pack

Mated to Team Shadow

Mated to the Pride

Taming Her Bears

Mated to the Clan

Protected by the Pack

Claimed by the Pack

Mates & Magic

The Sharing Spell

The Spell's Price

Backfired Magic